All an

All and Nothing

Raksha Bharadia

Rupa & Co

Typeset by
Mindways Design
1410 Chiranjiv Tower
43 Nehru Place
New Delhi 110 019

Printed in India by
Nutech Photolithographers
B-240, Okhla Industrial Area, Phase-I,
New Delhi 110 020

To my husband Sanjeev and mamma. . . .

Contents

Acknowledgement

Rajat Poddar for the way each character came to be what it is, in our conversations. . .

Prologue
August 1995

Tina stood on the balcony of Pragya's apartment waiting for the phone to ring. The old-fashioned black instrument was at an arm's distance from where she stood, just inside the small, sparingly furnished living room. The sky outside was dark . . . seagulls, crows, pigeons flying above were just fleeting shadows. The notorious never-sleeping city seemed, at this early hour, uncannily asleep. Silence ruled in this otherwise so-noisy metropolis. But Tina's heart was somersaulting.

Her gaze lowered, drawn to a bright glow emanating from an inconspicuous corner. It seemed to be from a section of the Colaba coastline. Boat-shaped shadows appeared to be radiating out from the epicentre of the glow. Tina smiled to herself. Bombay was not asleep. It was only fitting that its original residents, the Koli fishermen of Kolbhat, were its earliest risers.

As she glanced at her watch, for the nth time, the telephone jangled. She sprang to answer it.

'Good morning, Aditya.'

'A very good morning to you, Tina. Ready? I'm nearly there.'

'Yup. Will be down in a minute.'

'Sure.'

It was an old building with an old elevator. She waited impatiently for it to answer her call, and sighed with exasperation as it made its stately descent. Tina would have perhaps left the elevator door ajar in her impatience but its persistent door-open alarm forced her to ensure its full closure.

Aditya was just getting out of his small white Santro when she flew into his arms. He held her in a tight hug and, as they kissed, his hands relieved her of her two packs: a small valise and a picnic basket.

'You seem to be good at multitasking, Mr Malik,' she teased.

'Perfected the art with practice.'

Tina smelt the peppermint in his breath and the pungent aroma of his aftershave. He was dressed with simple elegance: a white cotton t-shirt with Nike Sports emblazoned across the chest and Roberto Cavalli jeans.

They were on their way to Mahabaleshwar.

'So, Aditya, tell me more about this mysterious Uncle Jha.'

'He will not let you call him that. He is my mother's brother, much younger than Ma though. Never married. After my parents died in the crash, he kind of stepped in and filled the gap.'

'What does he do in Mahabaleshwar?'

'He is a writer and has a charming little cottage, very quaint. I have spent many vacations there. He is looking forward to seeing us.'

Us! Tina's cheeks coloured instantly. She peeked at Aditya to see if he had noticed, but his eyes were on the road. Tina quickly filled her own awkwardness with small nothings about Mahabaleshwar – strawberries, horses, valleys, the temple.

Outside, the dark sky turned crimson and then a bright yellow. They chit-chatted all the way. The picnic basket remained unopened in the backseat. Just as Tina was beginning to feel hungry, they reached the cottage.

Prashant, Aditya's Uncle Jha, was watering his chrysanthemums and came out to receive them.

'Nice to have you over, Tina. You are as pretty as Aditya had promised – prettier!'

'Thank you . . . Uncle.' Tina blushed.

'No uncle. For you I can be Prashant – but mind, only till you get to know me better. Then it will have to be Prats.' Prashant was tall, a good five feet eleven, agile and lithe. His face was radiant in the early morning sun and even though balding, came across as extremely handsome to Tina.

'Sure, Unc . . . Prashant.'

'That's better. And if I know Aditya well, he would not have stopped for a tea-break. You must be absolutely ravenous.' He looked at Aditya and raised one eyebrow; Tina smiled, not knowing what to say. Aditya defended himself, 'That is unfair, Prats. I asked her a couple of times but she declined, saying that 'tea' will be with you only.'

'Mmm. Do not indulge him so, dear Tina. Men should be kept on a tight leash. More lessons later. Breakfast for now.'

Aditya was right. I like him already.

A rough wooden table was laid in a corner of the small garden, under a banyan tree. After downing cups of *masala chai*, with *aloo paranthas* and *achar*, the trio retired to the living room which opened to a large verandah. Prashant lit his pipe as Aditya excused himself to finish a few calls.

'He enjoys showing off his latest toy, this mobile phone,' said Prashant. Aditya grinned and wandered off into the verandah.

'So you are from the land of Tagore and Ray. Charming! You know, Durga Puja is something I have always wanted to see with a local. Perhaps with such a charming guide, if you concede that is, I will surely make that long impending trip. Tell me, is it as majestic as the papers claim it is?' Prashant asked as he blew out a little smoke.

Tina and Prashant spoke of Calcutta and Tina waxed eloquent on the charms of this once great city. At Prashant's gentle prodding she told him about her love for photography and painting, about her other interests, her likes and dislikes. He himself was a well-informed and erudite person, a witty urbane conversationalist.

Then Aditya joined them and they decided to take a small tour of the hill station.

After a brief drive around Mahabaleshwar, Aditya drove through a brown wooden gate into a private driveway. The two-hundred metre odd stretch was covered with thick foliage on both sides; in flashes, Tina saw the structure of a majestic white bungalow and the generous sprawl of a splendid garden, not laid out in the organised European fashion, but with natural harmony. They pulled up at the portico which was a huge arch dome done in white marble. The watchman came running down and greeted Prashant.

They took a short tour of the house. Everything about the place charmed Tina; the thick cool Mahabaleshwar air which had got trapped inside and was content in its acquired home, the deep silence of the inner height, the heavy marble banisters that glided up with grace despite their weight, the deep brown wooden furniture in stark contrast against the pearl white marble all around. Tina had not noticed that Prashant had left their company. As they strolled onto the patio, with a full view of the garden, she found herself alone with Aditya.

'Whose house is this Aditya?' Tina asked turning to him, but the grandeur of the house paled in front of what she saw in his eyes.

Tina's heart began drumming in her ears.

'Tina, I have given the first instalment for this house. This divine palace needs its deity. Will you marry me?'

BOOK 1

BOOK I

1

'Bye, mommy! We'll miss you!' Shaswati and Tamanna waved out of the speeding car.

'Mommy loves her angels too,' Tina's voice threatened to give way, but thankfully, the car had already moved out of earshot. She allowed herself the indulgence as two big drops made their way down her soft, smooth skin, somewhat easing the constriction that had gripped her midriff since morning. More tears would have followed, but Tina had things to attend to.

Getting hold of herself, she punched Aditya's number on her cell phone and conveyed the necessary information. 'Kids have just left. They should be reaching in another ten minutes. The passports and other documents are in Shaswati's backpack.'

Aditya had a business meeting near the international airport; he would just leave earlier with the children and see them off. They were flying to London to visit Tina's sister. Unwittingly, he had made it easier for Tina.

She had been dreading this moment, unsure of herself in bidding the final goodbye -- what if she broke down and shattered into more fragments than she thought possible, what if her resolve melted in the warmth of motherhood, what if she couldn't really walk away, despite knowing that she must.

But none of those happened. Yet again, the same sense of calm swathed her. She knew that the journey she was to embark upon was bigger than everything that she had been in parts – Tina the mother, Tina the wife, Tina the besotted, Tina the lover.

She went back as the mistress of her home of nine years, for one last time.

In the bedroom Aditya and she had shared for nine years, her suitcase lay packed and ready on the bed: the only things she would take from this penthouse. There had been no dilemma or temptation. She had instinctively known what should go in; for the things that didn't, she felt no attachment.

She located the number she needed in the telephone index and dialled it from the little-used landline.

'This is Tina Malik. Please have your man collect four envelopes and a packet from my residence. The packet is for Mr Jha in Mahabaleshwar, to whom you have delivered before. They will be with my cook, who will pay your courier charges in cash.'

She called the cook and gave him the five envelopes with her instructions.

The chauffeur saluted as she stepped out from the foyer of the building. He took the suitcase from the servant.

Getting into the car she told him, 'Bombay VT.'

There was no lump that formed in her throat, her voice did not quiver or become heavy. She was sad, immeasurably so, yet she did not feel weak.

Once they were on their way, the chauffeur asked, 'Madam, will you be gone long?'

'I don't know when I will be back. If . . .'

She looked at her watch. Their flight would have left, Aditya would be alone. She typed out an SMS on her cell phone: *I'm leaving*. Once the message had been transmitted Tina switched off her cell phone.

2

Upasna kept falling in and out of a disturbed slumber even as she took the telephone calls from her husband Umesh and from the office. At 1 p.m., her half-open eyes chanced upon the alarm clock on Umesh's bedside table. Cocooned in her Jaipur *rajai*, she sighed. Turning around, she plucked a slim plastic folder emblazoned 'Sun Pharma' from her bedside table. She browsed through the three sheets it contained, for the third time that morning.

As Head of the HR department of the Delhi-based company, it was up to her to decide between the three prospective candidates. The decision had to be finalised that day. And she had two important emails to draft and shoot-off.

Upasna's eyelids drooped. Over the soft hum of the air-conditioner, she heard a knocking on the door. The maid again, for the fifth time that morning. First she had come wanting to know if Memsaab wanted breakfast in bed, then the juicer had again broken down, then the gardener was asking for money to buy *forat* for the plants, then she had come for the laundry.

'Come in, Lakshmi bai,' she called out to the maid. She got up. Every muscle in her body seemed to be protesting against the effort.

She pressed her shoulder as the maid entered.

'Should I get you the cold compress, Memsaab?'

What will a cold compress do? It is not just my body. My mind and soul are equally battered.

'No, Lakshmi bai. It isn't necessary. Is there anything else?'

'What should I prepare for Baba, Memsaab? He was angry yesterday with what I'd made.'

Shanay will be back soon. He will want to know why I'm not at work. He'll see my bruised face and again want an explanation. More lies.

'Make *chilli paneer* and fried rice for him. Ask the driver to get a block of choco-chips from Baskin and Robbins too.'

Even after getting her instructions, Lakshmi bai waited by the door. Upasna looked at her with weary but questioning eyes.

'Memsaab, since I have started replying to his kicks with slaps, he now at least thinks twice before making me the punching bag for all his frustrations.'

Saying so, she left the room before Upasna could respond. In actual fact, Upasna had never been able to respond to the astute woman's sharp comments.

Upasna avoided looking at herself in the mirror as she went past her dressing table on her way to the study. She took out her journal and began writing. She wrote furiously, with deep, angry strokes. And then the tears came. At last.

Her diary, the faithful friend and confidante, once again made space for her misery within its tear-stained pages and allowed Upasna to dissociate herself from her situation. They kept her pain safe within and readied Upasna for the placid, efficient facade she presented to the world.

Lakshmi bai came in with the cold compress that had been refused and Tina's letter. It read as the others.

Upasna read the letter at least a dozen times, after which she placed it carefully under the chart-paper in her almirah. Her pain was forgotten.

I must keep Umesh ignorant of this till the last day. I must not provoke his wrath in any way till then. I can't afford not to go. I don't want to go with a black eye or an arm in a sling. I can make this happen. I must make it there for Tinee!

3

Kriya glared at the laughing face.

One day the termites will get you! All that will remain of you will be sawdust!

The gleaming wooden statue of a Laughing Buddha continued to mock her from its corner in Kriya's office chamber, as it had done for the last six years. Kriya could not get rid of it. She had not even dared to move it to another, remoter location in the vastness of her studio, Elan. The statue was a gift from her father. Seven years ago he had himself fixed its position while examining the plans for the studio.

Usually the soft and mellifluous chords of the *santoor* would pipe into her office – as it would throughout Elan – and calm Kriya. But not today.

The walls of her large chamber were clad in different fabrics – crisp organzas, bright linens, soft silks, slippery nylons, airy crochets, smooth cottons, warm wools, and seductive crepes – offering myriad possibilities in terms of colour and styling. But today Kriya could not bring to life anything 'fine' and 'original' – as so often.

Her seventh attempt at a *ghagra-choli* set, for starlet Amola's Geet Sandhya had come to naught too. Kriya aimed the crumpled sheet screaming 'failure' at the wastebasket. Overflowing with her previous failed attempts, the smart, generously-sized steel bin too spat out this latest failure. The crumpled ball of paper rolled back towards her. Kriya picked it up and flattened it once again. Perhaps she had overlooked some good strokes that could be borrowed for her next sketch. But the unappealing cut and pallid colours offered no encouragement. Kriya found it impossible to gather the courage and spirit for an eighth attempt.

Why do I have this compelling need to check every once in a while, if 'it' is there? Why does this bother me still, after so many years? I should just instruct one of my design assistants to execute the job, spare myself this self-inflicted trauma.

Who in my team can best cater to Amola's very discerning palate?

As she stepped out of her office, the buzz of creativity enveloped her: soft rubbing of pencils on smooth white sheets; clack-clack of snipping scissors sliding gracefully through fabrics; the muted thuds of fabrics being deftly folded, rolled and draped over one another. Her team of twelve talented minds, selected by her from prestigious design institutes like NID, NIFT and Shrishti, went about their work effortlessly and efficiently, bringing individuality to otherwise similar fabrics. And she, the daughter of the illustrious Mr Kasthiya, most sought-after fashion designer of the country, had created nothing but mediocre ensembles. The only relief came from the fact that the world outside knew her as the brilliant daughter of a brilliant father. Few knew the dark secrets behind her success.

Her eyes fell on the latest issue of *Diva*, the currently best-selling fashion magazine, lying on the worktable. Picking it up, she returned to her own office. Perhaps a fresh idea could be gleaned from its glossy pages.

As she browsed through the magazine, there was a knock on the door and a peon entered with a sealed envelope. Kriya recognised Tina's flowing hand and immediately tore it open. She read through the short letter once and, folding it, put it in her bag. She flipped a page on her desk calendar and buzzed her personal assistant on the intercom.

'Make a note in my appointment diary that I will not be available on the 9th and 10th of July. It's a weekend. And. . .'

4

The deadline was the next morning. Manas's nicotine-stained fingers raced across the keyboard. '*Ja shala, akhoni tui potol tulli naki!*' The computer had got hung again. The ancient machine could not multitask the way his mind did. 'Thank you, Mr Charles Babbage!' Yes, machines too are prone to stress. He switched it off and went to fix himself some lemonade.

What Manas really wanted was chilled beer, but there wasn't any left. 'I guess it's better this way. The beer would have only made me drowsy and I really must get those articles finished.' He grimaced remembering the editor's stern admonitions. Just then he caught his reflection in the mirror. He rubbed his bristling chin. A week's growth. His naturally curly hair had matted, not having been shampooed in quite some time. His faded t-shirt could only have done justice to a painter with its numerous stains. But Manas knew nothing of brushwork. He was a writer, a freelancer.

'Oh, Gayatri! Look what has happened! Why did you have to walk out on me?'

Manas angrily turned away from the mirror and stomped his way through the small studio apartment, kicking aside the odd newspaper, magazine, empty beer bottle, unwashed clothes, etc., he encountered in his path.

'Damn!' There was no ice in the refrigerator. He had forgotten to refill the ice-tray. Dishes and utensils lay strewn on the counter-top and piled in the sink. He couldn't find a clean glass. With a sigh, he began washing a glass for his lemonade.

The doorbell rang. It was the postman bearing Tina's letter. Manas read it with a trembling hand. . . .

Dear Manas,

Thank you for being a part of my life . . . an integral one. You must have guessed that things were not so smooth at my end, and I believe I am not mistaken in thinking that you too have waged a huge inner war in which, whoever loses, the wounded is just you.

You have been on my mind a lot lately. I want a day from your life. Please be at my farmhouse at Mahabaleshwar on the 10th of July.

What for? You will have to come and find out. I will not plead that you must, but I know that you will.

Love, Tina

Manas immediately went to the computer, determined to get the articles finished. If the machine refused to cooperate he would do it the old fashioned way – with pen and paper. Then he would book his ticket for Mahabaleshwar.

5

'Samarpan' carved in silver stood chic against the faded black *kadappa* stone. The gate to the Agarwal residence was not made of stone but was perhaps equally solid; through it one could not spy the sprawling property. It is possible that every square metre of its vast grounds was landscaped. The postman handed Tina's letter for Poorvi to the gatekeeper. In due time the letter found its way to the main house, which was in an uproar. The sole male heir to the Agarwal fortune, Aman, was a year old today. A huge celebration was in progress.

Brightly coloured balloons in assorted shapes, multi-hued paper streamers, colourful paper lanterns, shiny stars made of metallic foil, adorned the walls and ceilings. Huge colour blow-ups of Aman hung amongst the decorations. Liveried staff rushed about with trays laden with sherbets and cold drinks, with silver dishes of snacks and eatables. Thus, the letter remained undelivered in the foyer while the party raged.

Toddlers and older children were aplenty -- accompanied by, or rather accompanying, maids and servants. But the younger guests were easily outnumbered by their adult peers -- women dressed in the latest Satya Pauls and Manish Malhotras, carrying purses clearly identifiable as Gucci's and Louis Vuittons; flashing solitaires, emeralds, topaz and other such gems and jewels complementing their designer outfits or carefully nurtured complexions. Even amongst these glitterati, Poorvi stood out.

Poorvi's husband Avinash was the elder son. As the senior daughter-in-law of the house and an aunt to Aman, Poorvi was playing her role of the gracious host to perfection.

'Hi, Ross. I am so glad you could make it. Did you try the tortilla chips? They are baked.'

'Yes, I did. One can't really tell. You must pass on the source to me. You know how uptight everyone is about eating healthy these days! Nice arrangements, Poorvi. Even though it is Aman's celebration everyone knows his mother is incapable of organising and managing these affairs. Look at the way the grandparents are drooling all over that lucky child!'

Bitch! I knew she would pass some cheeky remark. 'We all love Aman. He is so adorable.' Saying so, she excused herself and moved to another group.

'Shimona, what a lovely sari. . .'

Poorvi moved amongst the different groups, tending to them, enquiring about their little ones, making small conversation, sharing a laugh, and complimenting them on their jewellery or sari. Dressed in a deep brown georgette sari with soft gold work, long *jadtar* earrings and four-inch pointed heels, she herself looked no less than a model from a fashion magazine. Mother of eleven-year-old Aanya and five-year-old Tarana, Poorvi was adept in planning classy theme parties and executed them with perfection. For this celebration she had had to reluctantly indulge in her in-laws expression of love for their only grandson, hence the large blow-ups of Aman, which she herself considered quite loud and tasteless. They had mercifully left the menu entirely up to her, only requiring it to be as exotic as possible whatever the cost.

Poorvi was in fact known as a trendsetter in chalking out exotic menus. As could have been expected many of the guests were left guessing when it came to identifying the various cuisines on offer and felt unsure of how they should react to the strange tastes and flavours making their way to unaccustomed palates. 'Asparagus in this seems fresh and not tinned,' said one. 'Yes, I believe Poorvi had it flown in from Singapore,' said another. A third, overhearing them and seeing them swallow the luscious stalks, smiled and said, 'It's delicious, isn't it!' Both nodded their heads in unison. As the first two moved away she tittered and whispered to her companion, 'I am sure both hate the taste of asparagus, but alas! It's the in-thing and they have no choice but to swallow it down with the most joyful expression. Oh, isn't that baklava!'

Avinash was chatting with some of the men. Poorvi tried to look for her girls and make sure that they were not gorging themselves on cola. She found the little one on granddad's lap telling him about her latest escapade with a friend. Aanya and Tarana were definitely pampered and fussed over by both her in-laws, but Aman was clearly the favourite. Poorvi cringed every time she saw the unmistakable look of 'my-family-torch-bearer' in their eyes whenever they addressed Aman or spoke about him. It somehow rendered all their love for her daughters null. Who was she angry with? Herself, for not providing the Agarwal clan with an heir out of her womb? Or the little, adorable, round-eyed, curly-haired, affectionate Aman; who, with his first independent breath, burst the bubble of Poorvi's perfect and happy world of thirteen years? The mere sight of him reminded Poorvi of her 'incompleteness'.

She glanced at her watch. There was still some time before the cake would be cut. She quietly left the party.

Why does this seem unbearable today? The party's a grand success, no doubt about it. All know it's my doing. So what if it is for Aman? I can throw a grander party for Tarana. No one will say a thing. But how do I make them see my girls the same way they see Aman?

Poorvi went into the foyer and was just entering the lift when the servant acting as the doorman for this overly-busy day hastened after her. 'Madam, there is a letter for you.' Without glancing at it, Poorvi took the slim envelope.

Lost in unhappy thoughts she reached her room, shutting the door with a bang. Sitting on her bed she tried to calm herself. Poorvi's eyes chanced upon the envelope. A smile lit up her face as she recognised Tina's flowing hand. All else forgotten, she ripped open the envelope and read Tina's letter.

Poorvi did not return to the party. She would feign a migraine. That night, she told Avinash about her impending trip to Mahabaleshwar.

6

The night of the ninth found Upasna tossing and turning in bed. Her eyes would flutter open with the clicking on of the air-conditioner compressor and she would look at the silent alarm clock, see that it wasn't time, and again drift off to sleep. Finally, at four, she got up and switched off the alarm. At least Umesh would have no cause to grumble about his precious hours of much-deserved rest being disturbed. Leaving her house slippers by the bed, she padded out on bare feet, gently shutting the door behind her.

She made her way through the sleeping house to the kitchen. The only sounds intruding upon the silence were the noises of the machines.

As she went about preparing tea, the refrigerator gave its periodical bursts of *dhuks* and *rrrs*, the fan its even whirrs, and Upasna's irritation rose. The machines were the monarchs of the night. One was never conscious of their characteristic sounds during the day; but at night, they made their presence heard, not allowing the absolute silence she craved. She took her tea to the garden and sat on a sandstone bench – the bench Tina had liked so much visiting Upasna in Delhi. . . .

Upasna and Tina were cousins by blood, friends by choice. Both had grown up in Calcutta. Pre-teen doctor-doctor games and pillow fights gave way to teeny-bopper sharing of innermost thoughts and secrets. Upasna's parents were much more conservative than Tina's. As soon as Upasna came of marriageable age a suitable groom was found for her. The marriage was solemnised in Calcutta, a grand affair. Upasna and Tina hugged each other during the *vidai* and shed copious tears. Through her tears Upasna whispered to her cousin that she would soon enough find an equally suitable 'Delhite' for her. 'Will check out Umesh's friends for you, Tinee. Do not commit.'

The initial months after the marriage the two friends spoke frequently on the phone. With the passage of time the frequency declined. Sometimes Tina would call and Upasna would be too busy to take the call. At other times Upasna was in a rush and couldn't speak for long. Their conversation became more and more aloof, distant, rarely moving past 'how are you' and 'what's up?'. Though they attended key events in each other's lives, the close bond that they once shared was lost.

Upasna was unable to attend Tina's own marriage as there had been a marriage in Umesh's family at the same time, and not in Calcutta.

Upasna occasionally made business trips to Mumbai. Some of the trips were just morning-to-evening ones and left no time for socialising. A few entailed overnight stays. On some of these longer trips the cousins would meet but conversation never traversed private matters.

On one such trip Upasna came to Mumbai armed with a fresh wardrobe and a determination to have fun, away from Umesh. She called up Tina and specifically told her to arrange an evening with some peppy ladies. 'Let's have fun, Tinee!'

Tina organised a ladies-night-out at the Blue Frog, a swanky new nightclub in Mumbai, which was the latest rage with the happening people. Upasna arrived soon after Tina and for a few minutes the two were alone.

'My, Upi! You've really maintained yourself well. You sure look the svelte businesswoman!' Tina complimented.

'Perhaps some gymming, Tinee. And a new wardrobe for this special trip.'

Tina pinched the little flab that had persisted. 'Look at this mini tyre, Upi! Give me some tips please?'

'Nothing like a little misery to make one lose weight, you know,' Upasna said. They laughed. But Tina noticed that Upasna's eyes did not crinkle, the way they did when she really laughed.

The waiter intruded.

'One tequila, large, for me,' Upasna ordered.

'Make it two shots, then. This will set in the right mood straight away.' Tina seconded her, though she was more of a wine sipper.

As Tina attended to a call on her cell phone Upasna surveyed the scene. The club was fast filling up with well-dressed people – youngsters and the not-so-young – all sporting the latest in fashion. Ritu Kumar, Sabyasachi, JJ Valaya, and so many others were all well represented. Laughter and music mingled with the cacophony of conversation in different tongues. The DJ was perhaps the only shabbily dressed person, but even his sleeveless t-shirt and carefully torn jeans seemed chic as he confidently moved to his own hip-hop music. The bartender was flaunting his juggling skills, even though it seemed to Upasna that he had no audience. People were too busy drinking, smoking, chatting, dancing or, in a few cases, just sitting quietly lost in their own thoughts, perhaps waiting for their companions.

'Poorvi, here!' Tina yelled, waving enthusiastically.

Poorvi waved back and was making her way to their table. Tall and slender, she looked sexy in a figure-hugging Ted Baker evening dress. She recognised a few friends in-between and stopped to chat.

'Did I tell you? She married into a prominent family of Mumbai. They have a sea-facing bungalow on Breach Candy. Her hubby is good-looking and super decent too. Talk of marriage material, eh!' Tina gave a quick background run on Poorvi as they waited for her to join them.

'She looks gorgeous and happy. And confident,' replied Upasna, still studying Poorvi.

Tina told Upasna about the other ladies who were to join them.

'. . .You know, Upi, there's something that bothers me about Kamini. I haven't been able to figure it out exactly, but I feel there's something more than what one sees,' Tina said, almost in a whisper.

'Isn't that true for each of us. . . ?'

Before Tina could respond Poorvi reached their table and Tina made the introductions. Then the others started arriving and the party got going.

As was inevitable, the conversation soon veered to the subject of husbands. Tongues loosened with the alcohol – and the gay abandon with which each strove to enjoy the ladies-only evening – the women, except Tina and Upasna, became more frank and bold than they would perhaps have been on another evening. They plumbed their deepest chasms and spoke of the most intimate details of their lives.

'When I asked Karan why can't he ever be romantic without being sexual, he said, "It is a combined package, sweetie. Take one, get one free!"'

'One evening, entering our bedroom, I stepped on a rattle that had fallen from the crib and hurt myself. Avinash immediately sprang up and gave me a soothing foot rub. Of course, we had a steamy session – I had to reward his sensitivity! But in the morning when I tripped again, and looked at him for a repeat action, he said dryly, "Why can't you watch where you're going?"'

Tina smiled at Upasna. The others were laughing uproariously.

'Men, do they even know that life exists above their groins?'

'Yes, they have fire in their stomachs, too!'

'As long as they don't have to cook! Avinash doesn't know the difference between simmering and boiling and thinks he's a gastronome.'

Taken up with the heat of the moment Upasna lost all her restraint. Amidst all the cross-talk she blurted out: 'On our first night Umesh tripped on my slippers. He got up, came to me, and slapped me full on the face.'

As Upasna continued the chatter at the table came to a screeching halt.

'Yes, he beats me often and I hide it – at times under full sleeves, sometimes behind dark goggles. When I cannot, I say I tripped and hit my head on the wall or some furniture. Now, no one even lifts an eyebrow when they see a bruised cheek. Including me! Isn't that funny?'

Some stared open-mouthed at Upasna, some looked away. Tina looked as if a bolt of lightning had struck her. None knew what to say.

'Hey waiter, get me another shot.' Upasna hailed a passing waiter even as she went on with her uncharacteristic outburst.

'I had promised myself that I would not think of the battering. Not this evening. But, hey! Lighten-up guys! Everything is not lost. I'm here, fit as a fiddle, aren't I?'

Upasna lifted her empty miniature glass and raised a toast, 'To the resilient me! Or maybe I should say: to the re-silent me!'

No one moved or said a word. Upasna sucked at the lemon.

It was some time before Tina spoke. She looked at Upasna with deep pain in her eyes and asked, 'Why do you take it, Upi?'

The sounds of the machines were drowned out by the frenetically chirping birds.

What could you not take anymore, Tinee?

'Memsaab, Shanay baba is asking for you.'

Upasna started and looked about her. The sun was up. She looked at her wrist but she wasn't wearing her watch. She had better hurry or she would miss her flight to Mumbai.

7

Kriya had driven to Pune on Saturday the ninth to spend a day and a night there with her father. Now, the morning of the tenth, she was on her way to Mahabaleshwar.

The sun was rising over the plateau as Kriya's black Mercedes sped along the Satara road. It had rained during the night, but the sky was now clear, the air washed clean and dust-free, the monsoon breeze cool and refreshing. The leaves on the few trees lining the newly-widened road glistened with wetness. The driver, Patil, was relieved that this freshly-tarred road would have no potholes and thus no puddles that could cause him or, *Raam-Raam*, his mistress to get splashed by a speeding truck. Patil had been shocked when his mistress had asked him to shut-off the air-conditioner and lower all the windows soon after getting into the car. In all his years of driving her around Mumbai and Pune and in-between, she had never issued such a command, not even in the coldest weather. He knew it was not just the dust and pollution that she wanted to keep out, she didn't like her hair ruffled. In his rear-view mirror, he could see his mistress's always perfectly coiffed hair already tousled.

She seemed to be enjoying the cool monsoon breeze and was lost in thought.

Kriya was thinking about Tina's worrying disappearance. Upon receiving the letter, she had attempted to contact Tina, but without success.

Everyone seemed to know that she was fine, but where she was, no one had a clue. Her cellphone was switched off. The domestic staff at her residence didn't know where 'madam' was or when she would be back. Daughters had been sent off to her sister's place in London. Kriya had obtained the sister's number and called her up. She had no idea of Tina's whereabouts and didn't seem to think there was anything unusual about the absence. Shaswati had spoken to her and said 'Mummy is on a sab . . . sabbatical.' Next, she called Tina's parents. They had received a letter from Tina that had worried them greatly. The letter said that she was okay and needed some time to be by herself, 'how much' she couldn't tell yet. She had warned them her cellphone would be switched off. As a last resort, Kriya called Aditya. He was abrupt. He too had no idea where she could have gone. *He does not sound really ruffled. Tina was very unhappy because of him.* Kriya let out a deep sigh. Only Mahabaleshwar would have Tina's answers.

'Patil, how much further is it?'

'At least another hour, madam.'

She pressed the control that raised her window. Patil raised all the other windows and quietly switched on the air-conditioner.

Kriya took out a brush from her purse and started brushing her hair.

Tina. . .

Kriya had met Tina at the Mumbai Gymkhana Club. Tina's daughter Shaswati and Kriya's son Yash were the same age. Both took skating lessons at the club and the mothers waited alongside. Kriya, the more outgoing between the two, had initiated introductions. In Tina, Kriya found a mother-mate.

Yash was Kriya's only child and Kriya an obsessive mother. He was born premature and under-weight, and had been a delicate baby, prone to infections. After his first birthday Kriya moved to Mumbai from Pune, divorcing her husband. Yash's constitution miraculously strengthened with the move but Kriya remained obsessed with his health. During those early years she often interrupted meetings with her staff or with clients to call up home and enquire about Yash, or to issue instructions to his nanny. As he grew into a healthy and active child, the calls lessened but never really ceased. Yash had only to sneeze and Kriya would be in a tizzy. She insisted on being present when Yash went skating as she worried he would fall and hurt himself.

In Tina, Kriya found as compulsive and indulgent a mother as she was herself. Tina, whilst sharing similar fears, was more obsessed with Shaswati's 'development'. She ran alongside the child to make her gain speed in skating. Kriya often had occasion to laugh at Tina's attempts at 'broadening' her daughters' horizons – the books she bought them were sometimes inappropriate for their ages.

The two of them started meeting without the children. At first, their discussions centred on the children – home remedies, diet, schools, books, and so on. As they became more and more comfortable with each other, personal matters also came to be discussed – husband (in Kriya's case, in the past tense), domestic staff, doctors, friends. . . .

'. . . and so I gave her the month's salary and asked her not to return.' Kriya said during one of their coffee meets.

'But you yourself said that she was honest and hard-working. She needed that job with you Kriya, you are a good paymaster.

Maybe attending that wedding was important to her.' Tina spoke in defence of Kriya's maid.

'Either you achieve a state where you can set your terms or else you work without asking questions, day and night! I manage people not just at home but at work too Tina, I cannot allow offs on such flimsy grounds. How about ordering a brownie? Kriya had made sure that Tina would leave the subject there.

Tina let it be.

Soon they were intimate friends opening their hearts out to each other, sometimes with perfect honesty, sometimes in a veiled fashion. What was left unsaid by one was understood by the other. Thus Kriya sensed Tina's insecurities and weaknesses, and Tina intuited Kriya's no-nonsense attitude and ruthless moods.

Kriya was a workaholic and busy with her studio Elan. It left little time for socialising beyond the needs of her business – which itself involved heavy partying, but with the fashion people. Aditya, Tina's husband, had expressed his dislike of the fashion industry in explicit terms. Thus over time, even though they lived in the same city, their interaction lessened. Occasionally they spoke on the phone, thus maintaining contact with each other.

Their last conversation had taken place several months earlier when Kriya casually called Tina. Sensing her friend's unhappiness Kriya forced Tina to confide in her. With her usual forthrightness she advised Tina to leave Aditya.

Now Kriya wondered – Had she?

The letter had arrived out of the blue. In it Kriya knew there was no subterfuge, no obfuscation. Tina had sensed, if not known, of Kriya's 'inner war', her mental turmoil.

You are right, Tina. I need help. And I know you do, too. . . .

8

Manas was snoozing on the bus to Mahabaleshwar, with a freshly shaved chin resting on his chest. The large lumbering vehicle went over a speed-breaker with a succession of judders, shaking him to wakefulness. As his bleary eyes fluttered open they fell on the piece of paper perched precariously at the edge of his shirt pocket. He pushed Tina's letter back into the pocket and checked to make sure his packet of Wills Navy Cut and matchbox had not slipped out.

How long had he known her? Almost ten years. They had met at Sanghavi's, when she had been taken on as a photographer. He was often teamed up with her for copywriting work. The two years she was away having babies had been the gap during which they had spoken only a few times. Then she had rejoined Sanghavi's.

Manas smiled to himself, recalling their first encounter. They had been teamed for a project.

To brainstorm upon it they fixed up a meeting for which he arrived nineteen minutes late. He smooth-talked the two other girls on the team into condoning his tardiness but Tina, he sensed, would be immune to his charm. As Tina was making her way out of the conference room Manas walked up to her.

'I am sorry, Tina. I have not been able to master the art of time management, though I try hard.' His tone was contrite.

'I know artists and writers too well to take serious offence at your lack of punctuality, Manas. Perhaps if you buzz when you are likely to be late. . .' Tina replied, smiling.

'I will, Tina. But for my appointments with you, I will try and be punctual.'

A no-nonsense woman, straightforward and clear.

Manas liked her immediately.

At first business-like and crisp, their relationship slowly deepened into a friendship. Both were impulsive, sensitive, intense, and perhaps a little crazy. When immersed in their work neither of them watched the clock; either of them could sense a moment's unrest in the other; when one drifted away in thoughts the other waited patiently, without irritation. The artist within gave them a unique understanding of the other. Manas often articulated exactly the theme and ethos of Tina's photographic creations -- without her having spoken a word. However complex Tina's themes, he unerringly suggested the right words. Tina rarely, if ever, declined Manas's recommendations. She had developed immense faith and confidence in Manas's creative abilities.

Gender did not play the devil between them; neither harboured romantic notions about the other.

Manas's world was his work, girlfriend Gayatri, and younger brother Aryan. His parents lived in Kolkata. Aryan was pursuing his medical studies in Mumbai, lived in a hostel, and visited Manas during weekends. Gayatri's middle-class Tamil family lived in Chennai. She had settled in Mumbai, working as a journalist with *Deccan Herald*.

Early in their collaboration, Manas told Tina of his live-in relationship with Gayatri.

Manas could barely manage his finances. He paid for his brother's education and sent some amount to his parents in Kolkata. Gayatri took care of the house rent for the flat they shared, while Manas met the other expenses. Though they could not afford Barista coffee, taxis, or the Sunday noon shows in the snazzy new multiplexes, Manas was happy and content with what he had. He loved Gayatri and she loved him. He enjoyed his job and it paid his bills.

Both Gayatri and Manas had strong and independent temperaments. They squabbled over small and large issues with equal passion. None would give in to the 'other' just because of their love. Every opinion, argument and debate had to be expressed vociferously or fought over tooth and nail. They had phases when they did not speak to each other for days together and they had phases when they did not step out of the house or without each other's company for up to a week at a time; making love, sharing conversations and the simple joy of each other's company.

Tina helped Manas make sense of the paranoia building in him due to the wilful Gayatri. She guided him through the complex workings of a woman's heart and thus understand Gayatri better.

Tina's *gyaan* about women made Manas realise that – When upset, women don't need advice; they crave a sympathetic listening ear and a strong shoulder to cry on.

However strong a relationship, every few days the man should verbally reaffirm his love to the woman.

Women scour the market for the tiniest possible box and the tiniest possible gift to go into it; when men receive the miniscule gift they should express amazement and great pleasure.

Women cry when viewing sentimental movies and remain unmoved in moments of pathos in their own lives.

Women ruminate over events much longer than men do. Wait patiently for Gayatri to get over what is bothering her. Never push her with 'you're over-reacting.'

And yet, all that they had shared, the intensity of their feelings for each other, was not enough in the end, to keep Manas and Gayatri together.

After seven years of living together, one Monday morning Gayatri packed her bags and left Mumbai. In an envelope she stowed several months' rent money which Manas found in his almirah.

Thirteen months earlier Tina had nursed him back to living. A severe asthmatic attack put him in the general ward of JJ Hospital. Broken and defeated, he insisted his attack was triggered by Gayatri's departure. Tina contended his smoking habit was the cause.

The last time we spoke I sensed your unhappiness. You rebuffed me. Why didn't you let me help you, Tina?

9

Poorvi was on her way to Mahabaleshwar. The car radio was tuned to a classical channel.

Na dhin dhin na
Na dhin dhin na
Na tin tin na
Na dhin dhin na

Poorvi's thoughts drifted back to the time she and Tina had shared at Anarth. . . .

Bipinbhai gave instructions to the motley bunch of the 'ladies' batch'. 'Take a break, girls. I will be back in five minutes. Revise *gat* in your minds till then.' Red-faced, panting and sweat-drenched after twenty minutes of continuous *tatkar*, they slowly made their way towards the cooler, their *ghungroos* tinkling melodiously.

Most of the women were in their thirties, a couple of years older, none younger.

Poorvi leant on Tina's arm, unstrapping a ghungroo. 'I will not be attending the next class, Tina. I have guests coming over.'

'Let me guess. They need your expert advice for trousseau shopping? Oh Poorvi, don't you tire of doing this day-in and day-out?' Tina asked, wiping her forehead with her dupatta.

'They are coming all the way from Tinsukhia. I have to help them out, Tina. They told Bina Mausi -- only Poorvi has taste in our family, only Poorvi knows what's fashionable and what's not. They hang on to every word I utter. It's very gratifying. It is a power, I tell you! Anyway, it's not as if Bipinbhai would miss my absence the way he would yours, Tina!'

'Oh! Come off it, Poorvi, not again!' Tina tried to look disapproving but burst out laughing as Poorvi got onto her favourite pastime -- mimicking Bipinbhai.

'Girls! You spend all your time giggling. Look at Tina, study her hand movements, she watches with care when I show. You all are not just *gopees*, you are Radha who is trying to keep others away from your Krishna. With your movements, you would not be able to entice a *dhobi* leave alone Krishna!'

The other ladies joined in.

'Enjoy the *thhat*. Remember, your face is the mirror of your soul. Get the right *bhava*. Tina always has it right.' 'Lose yourself in the *chakkars* . . . like Tina does.'

Tina was going red in the face.

'Stop it, all of you!'

Poorvi and Tina had known each other for nine long years. Poorvi was already a student at Anarth when Tina joined. Bipinbhai placed Tina in the same batch as her. They had become friends from Tina's very first day. Both enjoyed dancing, particularly the Jaipur Gharana style of Kathak taught by the guru.

Tina was unquestionably the uncontested best. Her aptitude and control over footwork amazed even the guru. She was the only one who could go through the entire twenty minutes of the tatkar practice session without a single break, not going offbeat even once or missing in-between steps.

After fifteen minutes, the tabla player would increase the tempo of the beat. Tina alone managed to keep up with him. The upper body had to be let loose, but not sagging; each foot had to come down with uniform pressure to create evenness with the sound that the ghungroos produced, thigh movement had to be clear and pronounced, but the upper body was not to carry the ripple effect of that deep thigh movement.

This expertise usually came after several years of practice, but Tina had mastered the skill unusually early, despite being irregular in attendance and often missing sessions of learning new *tukdas*.

Poorvi was well used to Tina's end moment SOS calls requesting her to come early to Anarth and teach her the tukdas and *baats*. Tina in turn helped Poorvi work on her hand movements. Though Tina's hand movements and footwork were perfect, she often goofed up in memory and sequencing.

And so, quite often as the entire class moved as one mass doing a chakkar backwards, Tina blissfully did the same in forward movement, sending the entire sequence into disarray. At times, engrossed in her own dancing, she would simply run into the student ahead of her. But whatever she did perform correctly was close to perfection. With the angle of her body during every *sam*, the right mix of sharpness and flow in her movements, balance in chakkars, a soft smiling expression, Tina could have been a professional.

Tina and Poorvi loved their twice-a-week Kathak sessions. The tabla beats, sound of ghungroos and rhythmic *bols* transported them to a different world, even if for just an hour. They uncloaked their multiple roles – wife, mother, daughter-in-law, homemaker,

problem-solver . . . and donned only that of an eager student,
concentrating on getting the nuances of the movements right.

'Wah!' Guru Bipinbhai said as all seven swayed in perfect
unison along the bol and each ended at *sam* at the precise fraction
of a second. '*Aaj aap sab ne bahut accha kiya.*'

The car drove into the petrol pump and brought Poorvi back
to the present. 'You should have got the tank filled yesterday itself,
Sudhir.' Poorvi climbed down to stretch her legs.

She remembered how they would often stand next to the car
after the dance class, at times for more than an hour, and talk
about their lives. They spoke about their domestic helps and their
tantrums; of the children – schools, examinations, extra-curricular
activities; the latest exhibitions in town or those forthcoming.
At times, when Tina was in a charitable mood, they would even
discuss fashion and high life, a topic that Poorvi enjoyed most.
These chats however never got into deep philosophical discussions
or life analysing conversations. But the two women had developed
such a rapport that through moods and nuances of manner and
behaviour, they communicated what they left unsaid. Poorvi was
not blind to the two contrasting women she saw live in Tina – one,
a bubbly, energetic woman, full of promise and life; another, a
woman who bordered frighteningly on depression. Yes, Poorvi knew
that the two sides existed simultaneously in Tina, even though
Tina never spoke directly about her deep melancholy. Sometimes,
Poorvi would detect the sombreness in her eyes on Tina's arrival at
Anarth, and would see it vanishing while Tina danced.

Yes, Tina had been unusually irregular of late and almost
always never stayed back to chat. And the last time we went out, I
did have to drag her out. Hmm . . . Now that I think of it, she was
so distant . . . I should have shed my inhibitions and extended a

deeper hand of friendship. But how could I, I was not even sure of who I was . . . even now, do I know, who I really am?

The car was in motion once again. 'How far are we now, Sudhir?'

'We will take less than an hour from here madam.'

I wonder what awaits me at Mahabaleshwar. . . .

10

Aditya reached Mahabaleshwar on the evening of the ninth, as Prashant had desired. The two dined alone at Prashant's place. It was a strained meal with little conversation. Aditya knew Prashant had summoned him to Mahabaleshwar at Tina's behest. He wished to know why. Prashant said they would discuss the matter over coffee. Aditya had no choice but to rein in his impatience.

After the meal ended they moved to the verandah. Prashant lit his pipe and Aditya his cigarette. For a few moments they sat in silence watching and listening to the monsoon rain that had begun to fall while they had been dining.

Prashant said, 'Now that it has rained today, tomorrow will be a fine day.'

Aditya shrugged.

Coffee was served. Aditya grimaced. The cups sat elegantly in a nook carved inside a wooden log, which served as a plate-cum-tray. It was a Tina creation. Some years back an old mango tree had succumbed to a storm around the time Tina had been re-furnishing their Mahabaleshwar home.

'Aditya, I must leave for Mahabaleshwar immediately. I just spoke to the caretaker. The storm was disastrous; the property is in a mess. You know what, our thirty year old mango tree fell. I'm taking Tamanna with me. Why don't you drive down tomorrow evening after Shaswati's school gets over? We can have a nice family weekend and also get things organised?'

That weekend resulted in a carpentry overdrive; numerous interesting wooden articles and artefacts were created. Two carpenters and a local sculptor were driven down on Saturday morning. Everyone except Aditya was into experimenting with chisel and hammer, mallet and saw, plane and spirit level. The stout trunk and thick branches of the old tree yielded six tables, four stools, a few benches, candle stands, picture frames, wall-hangings, vases, a doll house for the girls, small cabinets, and this very plate-cum-tray.

Tina was happiest when creating.

'Where *is* Tina, Prats?' Aditya asked.

'I don't know. All I know is that Tina wants to explore the world on her own for some time.'

'What! Are her friends aware that she will not be here?'

'I don't think so.'

'What will I tell them? This is bloody awkward, Prats!'

Prashant explained to him briefly Tina's instructions for the following day. As he had anticipated, Aditya was greatly upset about them, and threatened to return forthwith to Mumbai.

'I don't see why I have to go through with this, Prats!'

'If not for Tina, do it for me, Aditya.'

After much persuasion, and a little emotional blackmail by his only living kin, his steadfast guardian, friend, mentor -- for Prashant had been all of these to him during the lonely years of childhood and youth – Aditya agreed to do as Prashant asked.

BOOK 2

11

When Aditya had met Tina, he had been living in Bombay for the last two years.

Fleeing from Bangalore he arrived in Bombay to join Soft Solutions Ltd, a well-established, fast-growing and professionally-run company, as a mid-level executive. His goal was clear: to become one day it's President, if not its Managing Director.

He had little time during the day to think about anything other than work. By evening he would be too exhausted and drained to brood on the past.

Some evenings he partied with the office crowd and some he spent alone in his compact Marine Drive apartment, sitting on the breezy balcony, mesmerized by the waves beating their inevitable path on the shore. He took to reading: fast-paced novels, business books and journals, newsmagazines – he devoured them all. His lone servant kept him supplied with mugs of chilled beer. But he never drank in excess. When it grew dark, or when the weather wasn't right, he would ensconce himself in a comfortable sofa in the small living-cum-dining room and either read or surf the news and sports channels on television. Every morning he would jog on the wide pavement-promenade holding back the sea along the arc of Marine Drive.

Aditya shunned female company altogether and interacted with them only as much as work required. The office crowd he moved around with was exclusively male – young, ambitious go-getters. With his good looks, and well-cared for physique, he did attract the opposite sex; but his lack of a reciprocal interest soon drove the huntresses away, in search of other game. In the beginning there were whispers that perhaps he was gay. The men couldn't discern any such inclinations in him and the rumours soon dissipated. Whenever his physical needs became overbearing Aditya would seek release through discreet agencies which sent women to his apartment.

By the time he met Tina he had already become a senior executive in the flourishing company.

Pubbing with his friends he often raised a toast to his single, and thus less complicated, life: 'To us, who can see through the sham of love and marriage. Oh, how I love this freedom! It is perfect. I pay for what I need and get the best that money can buy!'

'Three cheers to us!' seconded his friend Praveen, himself a bachelor.

'Hey, marriage is not bad guys! It's nice to drive back home knowing someone's waiting for you. The acupressure I get from the soft hands of my little four-year old is mighty nice, you know.' Shodhan, though a regular at their stag nights, was very much a family man.

Aditya's eyes flared.

'Females, aah! I agree the little ones are lovable. But once they grow up, they can screw the shit out of you! With due respect to your wife, Shodhan, I stand for being single and unattached. Why do we go through the relationship game at all? Love is so overrated. I have never been as happy as I am now; free of the emotional crap we sell in the name of love.' There was venom in his voice.

'Amen to that!'

Soon thereafter Aditya was on the balcony nursing his chilled beer and reading a novel. The intrigues and rapidly changing scenarios of the story failed to retain his interest. He let the book fall from his hands and looked out over the vast expanse of the Arabian Sea. Not too far out he spied a fishing boat. It seemed to have a crew of just two, a man and a woman.

A great feeling of emptiness assailed him.

Aditya was tired of the stories he had been telling himself. In reality, he felt incomplete. Getting sex for money satisfied his physical needs, but did not fulfil his emotional hunger. He wanted to come home to someone; someone who waited for his return in the evenings, who was interested in the little details of his life; someone who would welcome him in her arms with real affection, not feigned interest; someone who would give birth to his children. He yearned for a family, which fate had so cruelly deprived him of in his growing years.

Bereft of the delicate female touch, squeals of playing children, his bachelor apartment lacked their warmth and softness.

Dusk was falling over the Arabian Sea as Aditya dialled Prashant's number. They spoke.

'. . . at work, too, having a wife and a family will give me that extra edge of permanency that singles somehow lose out on. Our Board has approved the creation of a new post of Vice-President. I recently overheard our President say that the Vice-President of Soft Solutions will definitely be a family man and singles have far less compulsions, tend to be more exploratory with their career. He said singles can be bad investments.'

'The time has come to give life another shot in that field, Aditya.'

'This time, I will be more conservative in my choice, Prats.'

'All women are not Antara, Aditya.'

'I hope you are right.'

Aditya started asking women out. There was no dearth of them. As word got around he found himself flooded with invitations. In his mind the parameters were clear: a reasonably attractive woman, ready for marriage, not too liberated, and not particularly enamoured of the high life; once wooed, she would love him madly.

Over the next several weeks Aditya dated recklessly. Most lasted a single evening, a few stretched to a week, but none for the long haul. All had agreeable personas. Some, in fact, were downright ravishing. But behind the make-up Aditya perceived calculating minds. Many took to pursuing him. Whilst his Antara-battered ego received a boost he did not allow their flattery to cloud his judgment.

Chatting with Prashant he said, 'These metro-sexual women are charming and quite agreeable. But they all link permanent commitment with economics. It is my potential bank balance that interests them, the bloody mercenaries! When they start pursuing me I lose interest.'

Then Aditya met Tina at a party.

In her short white *kurti* and beige *churidar* she stood out. The majority of the women there were wearing fancy western-style dresses and designer outfits. She wore little or no make-up whilst the others had loads. For a long time Aditya watched her. For the better part of the evening she stayed by herself. A woman, whom Aditya vaguely recognised, frequently approached her with someone whom she would introduce and then herself wander off. Aditya noted Tina's quiet confidence and easy manner as she conversed with these people without making any effort to hold on to them. Some who wanted to stay on unnecessarily, would be rebuffed gently by Tina, or she herself would just move on. She sipped her Pina Colada unapologetically amidst loud tequila shots and would have looked like a fish out of water, had it not been for the amused half-smile Aditya perceived on her face.

Her white dupatta slipped off a shoulder. The silky cloth had been hiding the lovely curve of her breasts under the tight kurti. She had shapely arms and her skin was soft and smooth, the colour of deep golden wheat. He felt a sudden urge to smell her skin. Her chest heaved as she broke into a small laugh.

She is surely not from Bombay. I must get introduced to her.

Aditya sought out the host.

'Oh, that's Pragya's friend from Bengal. Her name is Tina. She's an artist, a photographer. She has an exhibition on at the Triveni along with others from there. She's charming. Come, I'll introduce you to her.'

He introduced Aditya as a top-level executive in one of Bombay's most successful IT companies and then allowed himself to be drawn away.

Their interaction continued over the dinner that followed the cocktails and drinks. The friend, Pragya, also knew Aditya casually and was quite happy to leave the two of them on their own. Aditya himself did not allow any one to stick to them. Then the guests started leaving as the party wound down.

'It was nice meeting you, Aditya. If you have the time, do drop by the gallery. Well, one comes there to see the artwork, but maybe we can make an exception for you.' Her smile was accompanied by a naughty twinkle, and Aditya found himself going red.

'Uh . . . well . . . mmmm . . . I did not mean to stare . . . uhhh.'

'The exhibition is on for another week. See you.'

He was at the gallery the next evening. She gave him a guided tour of the exhibition, explaining in detail the intricacies of the displayed works, hers as well as of the other artists. He enjoyed her unassuming air and liked the dignity with which she carried herself.

'I would like to buy one of your works, Tina, the one of the woman set against that stony landscape. It would give the right touch to my no-woman house.'

'Hey! No formalities, Aditya! I'm glad you dropped by. You don't need to buy anything, really!'

'Except that I want to. I also want to invite you for dinner tonight.'

To Aditya, Tina seemed a little taken aback. She stood still, without a response, and Aditya hastened to ease the awkward pause with, 'You can say 'no', really. . .'

Tina cut him. 'Except that I don't want to. Dinner sounds great!'

They had dinner at the coffee shop of the Taj, in Colaba. The meal dragged well into the middle of the night when they felt the need to stretch their legs. They strolled on the promenade around the Gateway of India and in front of the renowned hotel.

Aditya told her about his school and MBA days, unpalatable hostel food, the constant need for budgeting and laundry, greasing up to teachers and then professors; Tina spoke of her orderly home with extended family where everything was well taken care of.

As the first light of the morning sun bathed the Gateway and the stately façade of the Taj, they sat on the parapet built at the edge sipping hot tea bought from a *kettlywallah*. Morning walkers passed by. Aditya and Tina were quite unmindful of the stares they attracted.

'I guess that's twenty-four hours of no-sleep,' she said hugging her cup.

'Do you mind it?' he asked, looking into her eyes.

'Does it seem as if I mind?' she teased and then broke into her soft smile, which Aditya found so endearing.

They finally parted after a breakfast of omelette at the Taj Coffee Shop once again.

'Do you think you can stay up another night, madam?'

'Well, I'm open to persuasion. . .'

'I know this place that serves the most divine pasta. Would dinner at La Italiana be convincing enough?'

'Yes, only if I'm allowed to take the tab.'

'I cannot allow my guests to pay and put at stake the reputation of the financial capital of our country, can I?'

'You got me. Let us see how different Bombay men are from Calcutta men.'

I like her. I am sure she likes me too.

12

Tina was staying with her friend Pragya in a Colaba apartment very near the Taj. The live-in maid who answered the door-bell didn't seem to find anything out of the ordinary in Tina's return after a night out. Tina scribbled a short note and left it with the maid, to be given to Pragya when she woke up. In it she requested Pragya to inform the gallery that she would not be going there that morning. She was a little peaked and intended to sleep through the morning.

At 1 p.m. her alarm went off. Opening her eyes the first thing she saw was the enormous bouquet of white orchids. A card lay propped on it. Beside it was a box. Her heart missed a beat. They had to be from Aditya. She got up excitedly. It was the first time a man had sent her flowers. The box turned out to be Godiva chocolates – all hazelnut, as she had told Aditya of her particular fondness for them. The card read: Thank you for the most beautiful evening of my life.

Tina spent the afternoon at the gallery and in the evening left early. She had not been able to stop thinking about Aditya and their long hours together. She looked forward to the coming dinner with eager anticipation.

Over pasta and wine they discussed each other's tastes and discovered many shared likes and dislikes. Over coffee and dessert they spoke about music and literature and discovered they had little in common. Aditya preferred racy novels and Tina shunned them, preferring biographies and philosophy, basically non-fiction which Aditya never touched. He did read the odd business-related best-sellers. Aditya had no interest in lyrics and listened to music only as an add-on to other activities. Tina loved varied genres of music and adored *ghazals* and *sufi sangeet*. They laughed off the differences.

Around midnight they left La Italiana and Aditya drove her around Bombay showing her various landmarks. They wound up at the Gateway of India again, sitting on the steps of Gateway of India and watching the ships and boats dotting the endless expanse. Even at 1 a.m. the place was abuzz with people and activity. Lovers, groups of friends, even a family or two idled around the massive stony surface enjoying the space and time.

Tina spoke of people she held dear, family members and friends, and of the things that never failed to bring joy in her life. 'Bombay seems to be topping that list now Mr Malik, quite unfaithful of me considering I have been here for just about three days,' she said, looking him full in the eye with that little twinkle.

Aditya took her to Haji Ali next; they sipped fresh watermelon juice amidst Tina's chatter about the Hooghly and the great yacht parties that the Calcutta elite threw – except 'the Calcuttans can't let their hair down as Bombayites can.'

'I can see that my city has charmed you, Tina,' Aditya said.

'City and its people,' she said smiling once again with that little spark in her eyes.

'Well this Bombaia will definitely try to live up to your faith,' he said, bowing to her. They laughed together.

Finally Aditya dropped her home at three in the morning, promising to meet up for lunch the following day.

That afternoon Aditya told Tina about Antara.

'I loved her deeply but she left me. She was ambitious and our conflicting needs from life resulted in our break-up and divorce. I thought I'd never be able to trust another woman again. You've changed that, Tina.'

'I have never loved another, Aditya' Tina said. Aditya scooped her in his arms and Tina had her first ever full kiss with Aditya that afternoon.

In the evening they went dancing to a city discotheque. Aditya was an adequate dancer whilst Tina danced with abandon. Some in the crowd made bold to urge Tina for a dance but she declined them all with a smile or a laugh.

The next day, Friday, Aditya had a busy work schedule so they arranged to meet in the late evening. A friend of Aditya's was having a party at his apartment. Tina charmed his friends and during the course of the evening Aditya received several compliments on his 'choice'.

Saturday they roamed around, drank sugarcane juice and ate *vada pav* at roadside stalls; browsed music at Rhythm House; shopped on Fashion Street. Tina bought Aditya a shirt and he bought her a leather sling bag. While Aditya went to meet someone in the afternoon at the Taj, Tina browsed at the book-shop. That evening they again went dancing. Dropping her home Aditya announced that Sunday they were going on a day trip.

'There is someone special I want you to meet in Mahabaleshwar. He has been my anchor since the death of my parents. And I also want to show you something.'

The rest of her stay in Bombay was a series of more 'firsts' for Tina. She experienced eternity in his kisses, the sweet pleasure and helplessness in the way her body responded to his touch, dancing without inhibitions in nightclubs, dining at the top-end restaurants or eating *vada-pav* at a corner stall, shopping at crossroads, sunsets on the beach, hours of talk and more talk.

13

'I have finally, finally met my Prince Charming. He proposed marriage in Mahabaleshwar, Pragya, and I have said "Yes!", I am in love! And it is as beautiful as I had read in books.'

'But you have known him just a few days!'

'Exactly, Pragya! No one has made me feel this way before, not even after a month of showering their attention and awe. Aditya is intense, intelligent, successful and doting. It is not just about the body for him. He wants my soul and mind too. You know -- he's been married once. She left him for greener pastures when he was just a low-level executive.'

'He is a divorcee?'

'Yes. Don't you see . . . I have been entrusted with this? I have to soothe his aching heart, heal him, and undo whatever pain that other woman inflicted upon him. I have to show him that all women are not Antara. He has picked me Pragya, and I love him. This is my destiny; he is what I have been waiting for. You know what! When Aditya spoke of Antara he said it was going to be the first and last time we would be talking about her. She is a closed chapter for him. She is history.'

'But Tina, I still can't understand why you would settle for someone who has already been in a marriage? You are beautiful, smart, and eligible from all angles…'

'I'm 24, Pragya. I've never been in love before. This is the first time my heart has thumped like this. Papa always teased me saying my Prince Charming did not exist. He does, now! Aditya will be down next week to meet them.'

Pragya smiled. *She looks so happy and radiant with love! Perhaps it is the real thing.*

'Silly girl! Pragya, you have to be in love to know how I'm feeling this moment. Look at this flower! For me it's more beautiful today . . . because I'm in love with Aditya. The hard marble under my feet is caressing me since morning because I'm special, because Aditya values me. Look at the sun! It's shining brightly because it knows I'm in love. Look at the sky, the clouds . . . the infinity they project symbolizes my happiness at this moment. Even if I die this moment I would not regret it, for I have felt love . . . How can this not be love, my dear Pragya? How could this be anything other than love? Aditya is what I have been waiting for. I know it as I know I am Tina.'

Pragya let go off her misgivings and joined her friend in a waltz around the room.

Aditya was at the airport to see Tina off.

'See you soon, sweetheart,' he called after her. *Tina will do me good. In time I will learn to love her.*

14

Aditya and Tina were married in a simple ceremony in Calcutta. Aditya was too busy to go for a honeymoon. He said they would have their honeymoon in Bombay.

They returned to Bombay to Aditya's new company-provided lavish apartment in the Breach Candy area. He had been promoted to Vice-President.

A few days later they had a small reception dinner at home for Aditya's colleagues. Tina's friend, Pragya, had moved out of Bombay having taken up a new job in another city. Prashant was present.

Toasting Tina with a glass of wine, he said, 'You seem to be Aditya's lucky mascot, beautiful lady.' Aditya too raised his glass of Black Label, soda and ice, to Tina. He said 'She sure is!'

Tina looked resplendent in a peacock-blue Ravi Arora sari that was part of her trousseau. She laughed and said 'I can't thank my gods enough for blessing me with the gift of Aditya's love. I hope and pray I always remain a source of joy and happiness for him. In his happiness lies mine.'

'Well said!' This was the President of the Company and Aditya's boss.

After the bigwigs had departed, Aditya and his cronies settled down for an evening of banter. Tina was busy elsewhere in the apartment with post-party chores. Prashant had retired to the guest bedroom for the night.

'Hey, Aditya, does she have a younger sister I can marry?' asked Praveen mischievously.

'Well-well! Change is certainly in the air! I got married, Bombay becomes Mumbai, and Praveen – the bachelor – wants to get married! I thought you were a die-hard bachelor, Praveen! And what about Julie? Isn't she your current girlfriend?' asked Aditya.

'Oh, we all thought of you too as a sure single man, Aditya. The gracious Tina causes people to reassess the joys of marriage. And Julie is history – caught her cheating on me. Not that I did not have my share of one-night-stands, too!' Praveen winked and hi-fived Aditya. 'Now, with a girl like Tina, I would be sure of her fidelity. And she would help me stick to mine! A guy has to settle down at some point in life, right? I just want to be sure that my girl isn't the sort that would dial my best friend the moment I was out of the door,' he said with a laugh.

To Aditya, Praveen's laughter seemed false. It did not reach the eyes.

His gaze went to Tina, who happened to be hurrying by. Yes, he was indeed lucky to find a girl like her and be the envy of his friends. She was a trophy wife in that respect, but he perceived a greater role for her. Societal necessities had had a crucial bearing on his decision, but his personal needs had still been paramount. With her he would have children, a family, a sense of the home he had never had. His life would be stable, not turbulent – as his life with Antara had been.

Entering the third month after their marriage, the euphoria of honeymooning stabilised and settled into a harmonious marital equilibrium. The spate of parties and dinners gave way to quiet, peaceful evenings spent at home.

'It is nice to be with each other in pajamas at eight in the evening and not think of what to wear to yet another boring dinner party, Aditya,' Tina said, sinking into Aditya's waiting arms. He smiled at her.

She does not crave male attention as Antara did. Aditya could read Tina like a book.

Tina was new to the world of romantic love and it enthralled her. She wanted nothing more from life other than to go on loving him. She made Aditya's world her own universe. He, of course, was its epicentre; she, his satellite. People, things, activities held meaning for her only if they meant something to Aditya. She painted sporadically. Her camera remained within its case. She never felt an urge to write, not even in her diary. She rarely thought of her family and friends back in Calcutta. Her very personality dissolved in his. If at all the Tina in her mattered, it related only to the facets Aditya found appealing. She took great care in her toilet and dressing as Aditya found meaning in her body and took pleasure in her appearance.

During the hours he spent at his office, she pined for him and planned for the time he would be back home in the evening. She made full use of the knowledge she had acquired of his likes and dislikes during their brief but intense courtship. His old servant, who could have been a great help to her, had vanished. Now, in the new apartment, they had a new cook-cum-servant and a new maid. Aditya had very set habits and very particular likes and dislikes. She trained her staff to cater to his exacting needs, most of which she discovered only in the first few days of living together. Chilled beer must be served in a pre-chilled mug wrapped in a tissue. Carrot, cucumber and radish must be diced lengthwise, not too-thick or thin, and served with the beer. The toiletries must always be placed in a particular order on the bathroom shelf. His shirts and trousers must always be perfectly pressed.

One evening, as they sat together on the windowsill overlooking the ocean, with drinks in their hands, she said dreamily snuggling closer to him, 'You are what I have waited for since I was fifteen, Aditya. No one has made me feel the way you have. I think I loved you from the first day I met you.'

Aditya looked down at her with deep fondness. He was indeed enjoying this expression of love. It salved his wounds, made them less hurting. In every aspect Tina was better than Antara – looks, intelligence, fidelity, depth. Tina was his due. And he had come to care for this child-like girl he was holding in his arms. He felt the stirrings of love in himself too.

'Thank you, Tina,' he whispered in her ears as he nestled deeper into the nape of her neck.

'Oh, Aditya! All your pains are now mine. I promise you, I will make you forget Antara. I will make up for the heartache she has made you go through.'

Aditya went rigid.

He withdrew himself in one sharp movement and walked to the balcony, closing the door behind him.

I will make up for the heartache she has made you go through.

The words felt like acid-stings. He lit a Marlboro Lights. His face contorted in anger and humiliation.

I cannot escape Anatra. I will never be rid of her. She now lives with me – in Tina.

A little later he returned to the bedroom where Tina waited, confused, afraid and unsure. He went to the bathroom to brush for the night. Tina followed him and wrapped her arms around his back. He felt her tears wet his nightshirt.

'What's wrong, Aditya? Please tell me. Have I hurt you in anyway? You know I would never do that in my wildest dreams. You believe me, don't you? Turn around, Aditya. Look at me!' she begged.

He turned around and hugged her.

Why are his eyes so cold? Surely I'm imagining it. I'm in his arms, aren't I?

15

Tina's excited voice crackled through the phone, 'I got the job, Aditya! They have retained me as second-in-line to Pratap Sanghavi's right-hand photographer. I begin work from tomorrow. Isn't that great?'

'Very nice. Mmm . . . I will be home by seven and we will celebrate then. I am a little tied up right now, Tina. Can I call you back in a bit?'

Tina was not too dampened by Aditya's words. She was too elated for getting the coveted position. Feeling the need to share her joy with more people she called her parents in Calcutta and Prats in Mahabaleshwar. Her parents were pleased that she was going back to work. Prashant generously offered his house for photo-shoots.

'With some client picking up the roll costs I'd love to capture the enchanting cloud-hidden hills of Mahabaleshwar, especially during the monsoons. But be warned, Prats, we travel in crews of ten or more.'

'If they are as charming and intelligent as you then my house doors are more than open for them all.' There was genuine pride in his voice, in sharp contrast to Aditya's lukewarm response.

Maybe he was tied up in a meeting. I shouldn't have called on his cellphone.

She decided to complete her to-do list for the day. In Calcutta she had been a keen student of Kathak. Her old dance teacher had furnished a reference of a renowned dance school in Mumbai, Anarth, run by Guru Bipinbhai. She went and met him to explore the possibility of restarting Kathak. After a short try-out he accepted her as his *shishya*. To her delight, he said she could start that very day. The familiar mellifluous sounds of the ghungroo and the bols lifted her spirit.

That evening she was a bundle of excitement and prattled animatedly to Aditya about her productive day. Sanghavi's studio was a store-house of energy with an electrifying buzz. Bipinbhai had been pleased with her dancing. At Anarth she had also made her first friend in a new city: a young newly-married woman like herself. Poorvi was sweet, had panache, and was fun to be with.

'A dashing MBA hubby, sea-facing flat, job at Sanghavi's, Kathak; life does not come wrapped better than this, Mr Malik. I have so many plans with myself and your city, Mumbai!'

16

Aditya and Prashant spoke regularly on the phone. Either one or the other would call about once a fortnight.

'I think I am ready to start a family.'

'You've been married just six months! Enjoy each other for at least a year or two before you get into that business, Aditya.'

Aditya diverted the conversation to other subjects.

That night, lying in bed in each other's arms after a bout of love-making, Aditya said, 'Let's have a child.'

'So soon! Don't you think that would be rushing things, Aditya?' uttered the surprised Tina.

'I am already thirty-two, Tina. . .'

'I don't think a child is a good idea at this point. Surely we can wait another year!'

'We start trying for a child now and it will arrive in a year. I cannot wait two years!' Aditya's tone had become raspy.

'I've just started work at Sanghavi's. I become pregnant now and in a few months I won't be able to go for location shoots. My Kathak, which I've just restarted, will also stop. No, Aditya, I'm not ready!' Tina exclaimed.

It was the first time the ever-pliable Tina had refused anything to Aditya. He extricated his arms from around Tina, sat up on the bed, and lit a cigarette. Tina was staring at the wall. If she had been looking at him she would perhaps have seen the slight quiver in the hand that held the smoking stick. Feeling that she may have sounded a little harsh, Tina softened her tone and said in a placatory voice, 'We have to get to know each other fully before we bring a child into this world, Aditya. It's a big responsibility.'

'I know my responsibilities, Tina. I have a steady job. I am earning well. My prospects are excellent. We have known each other for almost a year. Our life is as stable as it can get. I really see no reason to wait any longer.' The curtness in Aditya's voice cut Tina to the quick.

'And I do! I'm certainly not ready for that kind of responsibility. It's not that I don't want kids. I do, but not just yet. Besides, Aditya, we have to get rid of our past baggage before we take such a big decision. I don't feel that you're ready, even though you may think you are.' A little belligerence had made its way into Tina's tone as well.

Aditya's face hardened. He crushed the cigarette in an ashtray lying on his bedside table. When he spoke his tone was cold.

'Is it constitutionally impossible for you to talk about anything fundamental without dragging my past marriage into it? If you do not want to have a child, because you want your freedom or whatever goddamn reasons you have, have the guts to own up and say so. Don't hide under false pretexts! Don't pass the buck! People with false pretences, especially those who use others as a pretext, disgust me!'

He flung the blanket away and stalked out of the room. Tina followed him.

'You are obviously still not over Antara walking out on you. She still colours all your reactions. Even your desires! Do you think I'm stupid enough not to see why you want this child? You think a child will secure me to you. But you don't need to, Aditya. I'm not Antara! I won't walk away as she did. Can't you see that I love you?'

Suppressing her own flaring anger, she continued.

'I don't want to hurt you, Aditya. But you really need to let go of Antara, to extinguish your painful memories of her. Your big male ego is clouding your mind. Our relationship is still nascent. This Antara baggage you carry is poisoning it. Don't do this please, Aditya!'

'What makes you such an expert on the human psyche, darling? As I can recall, psychology was not your subject; you graduated in fine arts. Your art career was not really taking-off. You were on the hunt for a providing husband, admit it! I am fulfilling my role, fulfil yours!'

'That hurt, Aditya. That hurt very much. We love each other. Isn't that the reason we decided to be together?'

Tina was trembling. A poignant panic had begun to accumulate in her chest, which shot like a physical pain through her entire body. She saw his eyes and knew what would follow.

'Aah, Love! Spare me that word. You women are all the same: going ballistic at the drop of a hat, using emotions to achieve your twisted goals. Yes, Antara was a selfish bitch and a social climber. You, Miss Goody-two-shoes, are no better! In my grief you found your life mission and called it 'love'. What a nice elevating social wrap! At every available opportunity you throw my failure at me. Is that love? Sick! But you know what, I am a bigger fucker than both of you; I believed in your innocence. Perhaps I deserve you . . .'

Tina looked at Aditya's contorted face in intensified shock.

The man I married was suave, agreeable, balanced. This person is a raging egoist!

She fought for composure.

'Aditya, please stop it. What's got into you? Your words hurt so. . .'

Aditya cut her mid-sentence.

'Hurt eh? You have no idea how terrible hurt can be. You have no idea at all!'

She tried to sound firm, though every fibre in her body threatened to give way to the tears she was struggling to hold back.

'Yes, I've no idea what your version of 'hurt' is, or why you're doing this to us, but I do know that we are not yet ready to bring a child into this world.'

'Is that your final answer?'

'Yes.'

'We will see.'

They slept in separate rooms that night. When she had no more tears left to shed Tina sat down with her diary – the diary she had deserted since her marriage. Over the years, the words that had flowed into her diaries, had helped Tina through many a crisis, helped clear her doubts and reach crucial decisions. But no crisis ever had been so serious, no doubts had ever been so traumatic, and in her great confusion, decision was not what she sought. What she hankered for was understanding, comprehension. She was sure she had mishandled the situation.

The malaise is much deeper than I had ever thought possible. His failure with this Antara eats him up, obsesses him. He is a passionate, wilful, hot-tempered and intense man,; but he can be so caring, considerate and loving. Most times he is so. I must be more patient and understanding, more careful with my words. He loves me in his own way – well, maybe not; not till he lets go of this horrible woman. I must warm him again to 'love' . . . There is no other option. He is the first man I have cared for in my life. I have to make this work.

Tina was prepared for a backlash – cutting remarks, arguments, perhaps another bitter fight. But Aditya simply built a moat around himself.

He left early for work. More often than not he was too busy to take her calls. When he spoke, his tone was curt, answers monosyllabic. He came home late, after dinner, and went straight to bed.

Two nights running he curled up with his back to her, inched away from her touch. Once, he harshly flung away her caressing hands.

Two days running her warm glances bounced right off him. If she tried to speak to him he either walked away without a word or answered with hurting brevity.

The third night following their exchange he returned home a little early.

Determined now to make him speak with her, she went to their room and found him packing a suitcase. The strain and tension that had accumulated steadily over the past days reached their zenith. A great panic gripped Tina.

'Where are you going? Are you leaving because of that one stupid argument?' Her chest heaved violently, her breath came fast and heavy, her tone was pitched, high-strung.

'I am going on official work,' he retorted brusquely.

'Where are you going? When will you be back? Why didn't you tell me about your trip? How can you leave like this? I can't believe this is happening to us!' Tina sat on the bed, covering her face with her palms. Sobs racked her body.

Aditya stopped his packing and sat next to her. A little more gently, he said, 'I will be back in two days.'

Tina looked at him through her tear-stained face. 'I want to come with you, please. I can't take this any more, Aditya. I cannot sit here in this house knowing that you will not return in the evening. I will die, Aditya! Can I come with you, please?'

'Tina, you promise me the world and I believe you. Yet when I ask you for one important thing, which doesn't happen to be on your current agenda, you say 'No' without a moment's hesitation. Why should I believe anything that you are telling me now? Give me one good reason why I should believe that the love that you swear by is what you say it is?'

As Aditya spoke, he held her in his arms. In that one gesture – more than in the calmness of his voice, its soft tone – Tina discerned the man she had fallen for, the man who had bowled her over so completely her first days in Bombay.

'Let us have a baby, Aditya. If that is what will convince you, so be it. We will do whatever you want. But please don't cut yourself off like this again. I had not anticipated having children so soon after marriage. Perhaps I should have given it more thought before saying No.'

'Oh, Tina! Thank you!' He hugged her and brushed away her tears with gentle hands. 'It will be all right, Tina. The baby will do us good. Trust me. But if you would rather wait. . .'

'No! I don't want to wait anymore.'

Aditya had left for the airport and Tina sat with her diary. The page before her was blank, as was her mind. She felt drained of all emotion, all thought. In time, she began: '*Dearest Diary, Aditya is right, what can be more beautiful than to become a mother. . .*'

At that same moment, Aditya sat ruminating as he was driven to the airport.

Fair/unfair, good/bad there is no point in berating myself over it? This is the reality: the way I feel is the way I feel. Oh, Tina! Innocent little baby, putty in my hands! I can mould you any way I like and you will be helpless. You see I am helpless too. I am Antara's creation.

17

Now that she had reconciled herself to the thought of an earlier motherhood than she had anticipated, Tina looked eagerly for the signs of pregnancy. But her periods occurred with clockwork precision. As the weeks went by, she thought more and more positively of the prospect of motherhood; the new life that would spring inside her would be part herself and part Aditya, a binding·force like no other. Once in a while she even chastised herself for not having agreed with Aditya's wishes earlier. He was basically a family-oriented man and, having lost his own parents at an early age, of course Aditya would want to start a family. Through her body Aditya would realise what he craved so much; it would smother Aditya's unhappy memories of his first marriage and strengthen theirs. He would again shower on her the attention he had shown during their brief courtship. The security the child will give him will make him softer, more relaxed. *He will learn to love again. . .*

Not one to live life in half measures, Tina gave herself fully to her new life in the 'dazzling' city of Mumbai.

She was working full-time for Sanghavi's. Her salary wasn't much but that mattered little to her. She enjoyed the challenge and vibrancy of the workplace. Bizarre ideas and random concepts were discussed with an open mind and an intensity that initially daunted her. In Calcutta, whatever little work experience she had garnered had been staid in comparison, even laid-back. Here there were fewer rules, but more accountability; less discipline, but more output. Here she was part of a team that worked with a zest and vigour that she had never thought possible. The work excited her; she felt useful and rejuvenated.

Tina welcomed the new friends that marriage and Mumbai gave her. Prashant – or Prats as she took to calling him – was her 'Krishna'; she could laugh, flirt and speak philosophy with him; within a short span of six months they forged a deep friendship. Manas, copywriter at Sanghavi's, was her male alter ego; intense and earnest, they complemented each other's skills and often emerged with winning solutions; she could converse with him in Bangla, which often proved useful as it assured them privacy – no one else in the office knew the language; and they shared a common craving for the *patali gud* that just wasn't available in Mumbai and could only be procured from Calcutta. Poorvi was a friend she had become very fond of, a walking-talking *Vogue* magazine, she regaled Tina with the doings of the glitterati of Mumbai; and educated Tina on the art of looking chic. Tina enjoyed the company of Aditya's colleagues, too; they were perky and fun, their wives simple and endearing.

Mumbai was a place where Tina felt she could be herself the most. It was wild and crazy compared to her quaint and cautious Calcutta. This city, it seemed, pushed its people to dream big; and then made them work with a mad energy to realise those dreams. After a grilling day at work, Mumbaikars – as they now called themselves – poured out of their homes to chill and party; in having fun they exhibited as much energy and innovation as they did in their workplaces. Mumbaikars exuded a sense of joie-de-vivre, an élan that restrained and conservative Calcutta had never shown. Projects or relationships – all moved at breakneck speed.

Every alternate weekend they drove down to Mahabaleshwar. Tina loved deliberating over every little corner of the blossoming villa and in bits and pieces turned the old Victorian structure into a warm, living weekend home.

Their first wedding anniversary neared. Twenty days before it they were dining alone at home, telling each other about their day.

'By the way, we will be celebrating our anniversary at the Taj. We have a suite for the night,' Aditya announced.

Tina was thrilled. During their hectic courtship they had visited it a number of times. 'Oh, Aditya! What a romantic thing to do! But won't it be very expensive? And our friends are sure to protest. Ketaki and Neena have been asking me about it. They're expecting us to have a party.'

'Don't be silly, darling! We will not be staying there overnight. The company has booked the suite for an overseas guest whose flight leaves late evening. As the hotel will anyway charge us for the night the President suggested I make use of it. He remembered it is my anniversary. We will ask Shodhan, Prahar, Praveen and all the rest to come over and we will have a bash.'

'Oh, is that it?' uttered Tina, trying to hide her disappointment.

A week before their anniversary day, Aditya informed Tina that the Taj programme was off. The overseas guest was not coming. Aditya would in fact have to fly to Munich to meet him. He would be leaving the night before their anniversary and returning after two days, maybe more.

Tina was alone on their first wedding anniversary.

That winter they drove down to Mahabaleshwer with a few friends for a private New Year Eve celebration. Prats too joined them for their 31st night celebrations. It was a rambunctious affair. The next afternoon the group lounged near the pool, enjoying the winter sun on their faces, barbecuing *paneer*, potatoes and chicken. Prats sat with his Kingfisher and pipe, listening quietly to the conversation jumping from one topic to another.

From light-hearted banter, the conversation moved on to terrorism and the alarming developments in Afghanistan. Inevitably the topic veered round to Pakistan and its support of the Kashmir insurgency. The leisurely afternoon provided the perfect setting to declaim their couch-patriotism.

'Those fellas think we're weak and timorous. Our politicians are much more than just that. They care a damn about the nation; only care about increasing their vote banks and swelling their hoards of cash. Expecting them to act decisively is foolish. We should hand over the country to our military,' said Prahar between huge gulps of chilled beer.

'I can't understand our meek approach. We know the forces funding the insurgents, yet we play the abominable cat and mouse game. We, with the third largest standing army in the world, behave like a bunch of eunuchs. Disgusting!' seconded Shodhan, slamming his glass down in righteous indignation.

'Yes, what we need is grit, military rule! Nothing less will save our country I tell you.'

'It is high time we answer them through actions rather than just words. Enough of dialogue!' exclaimed Ketaki, Prahar's wife.

'Tell me, what do they have to lose? Already on the brink of bankruptcy, with a sham of a democracy, a completely divided nation, what do they have to lose? In fact, they want to provoke us into a war. That way, the military will come into power and we will be worse off,' said Praveen, still a bachelor.

'Praveen, I agree with you. Can't we send our agents across covertly and destroy their camps? We should give them a dose of their own medicine, wage proxy wars as they have been doing. Why should we go to war and endanger innocent lives, bring upon ourselves economic hardship and worldwide condemnation?' Tina said, her face animated.

Prats smiled. 'My little Ninja! We should elect you to Parliament and have you as our Minister of External Affairs. Cabinet rank.'

Before Tina could say anything, Aditya burst in.

'I second Tina on this matter. I also propose all the agents be women. Married ones. Scouting and suspecting comes naturally to them, they would not need much training. With years of practice of keeping tabs on their husbands. . .' Aditya hi-fived with a friend and all the men, save Prats, broke into peals of laughter.

'Their razor-sharp instincts, honed through years of practice, could be a potent weapon for our government. Neena even knows the perfumes my women colleagues use, and if I smell of anything unusual . . . wham!' Shodhan said. Neena threw a chicken bone at him, hurling abuses, while others told him that he had lost his evening points in that ill-made comment.

Politics took a backseat as the men strived to outdo each other in relating anecdotes of how wives constantly double-checked their husbands' whereabouts, even as they feigned disinterest.

'A friend told me that his wife once smelt a woman's perfume on his shirt and was a tigress in bed that night!'

'Aah, competition! Nothing better to bring the best out in a man -- oops, a woman!'

'He said he felt like a sheik in a harem. Only, it was a one-woman harem!'

'Talk about returns! Perhaps we too should try dabbing some exotic perfumes!' Aditya smirked.

'Amen to that.'

Tina, writhing inside, observed the women closely. They did protest against the nasty insults, gave disgruntled pseudo-hurt comebacks, yet she could see that they were not seriously offended.

Aditya's snide comments had really offended her. She simmered.

They broke up for an afternoon siesta. Out of earshot of the others, she charged Aditya. 'What tab have I kept on you? How can YOU think like an MCP, Aditya?'

Aditya had downed a couple of Bloody Marys and a beer during the afternoon sojourn; this, after the hangover of the previous night's binge.

'Oh come on, Tina! That was just fun. You should not take it personally.' As he spoke, he slipped his hand under her shirt. The patronising tone, the lustful glazed look in his eyes, made Tina feel more degraded and cheap than his earlier utterances. She threw his hand away violently.

'Aditya, I'm serious. What do you think women are good for? To screw at will while they manage the homes and children of philandering husbands? Disgusting!'

'Philandering! What crap! You are the one who can't stop jabbering about your 'creative' Manas. And you have the guts to call me philandering!'

'What's gotten into you? How can you even think like this? Manas is a colleague of mine. He has a girlfriend, Aditya. We have nothing between us.'

'Of course I know you have nothing with him. He does not have the *moolah* for you to have something with him! That *jholawala* uses his girlfriend's pay cheque to fill his rent bills.'

Tina was too shocked to respond.

'And why aren't you getting pregnant? We have been trying for over six months now. Are you secretly gulping pills to avert a pregnancy? I will not be fooled by another woman ever again, Tina. I warn you!'

All of Tina's irritation vanished. Aditya's afternoon utterances were insignificant in the face of this onslaught.

'I want the baby as much as you do, Aditya. I am not taking any pills. I pity you for the faith you have in me.' Tina's voice cracked as she said this.

'Don't pity me, pity yourself! At least I have the guts to say exactly what I want, what I feel. You think me a fool! I can see how a baby would interfere with your newfound freedom, with that measly fifteen-grand job of yours – and your time with that *fakkad* Manas, of course!'

'Yes, I relish my work and I like Manas very much too, though not in the way you think. Manas respects women and does not chunk them in one category as you do'.

'Sure, he respects women! How else will he get them to like him?'

A sudden urge to hurt him possessed Tina.

'Maybe that's the way he gets his women, but they don't leave him the way Antara left you!'

The moment the words were out she regretted them.

'For your information, there are many women dying to be in my bed, far more attractive and interesting than you, if not Antara. I am sure they would be better in bed too, and maybe it is time I found out.' Aditya's tone was icy. He gave Tina no opportunity to salvage the situation. Even as she stood, stunned and shocked – more with herself than with Aditya – he stalked off.

As he disappeared round a corner of the verandah she saw Prats. In his hand he held Tina's sunglasses. From the pained expression on his face Tina knew he had heard everything.

'Tell me Prats, is he that bad or was it the alcohol?'

'The alcohol, I'm sure. Aditya is not much of a drinking man. And you shouldn't have made that reference of Antara. Hitting below the belt. Let us take a walk outside.'

Prashant and Tina made their way towards a nearby hill. None said a word.

'Pills', 'Manas', 'measly', 'fool', 'work', Tina's mind kept repeating random words from the outburst. As she reached the summit the words organised themselves in her mind: *Aditya does not love me. He never did. It was always about him.*

She stood at the edge and stared at the abyss below.

'Tina! Get away from there! You have had one husband-wife tiff, that's all!' He pulled Tina down on the grass.

A thorn pricked her and she gave in to the tears she had held back for long.

'You should have warned me about him. You knew it, Prats! Why didn't you tell me? What do I do with him? With myself?'

Prashant just held her close, saying nothing. When her sobs had subsided, he spoke.

'Aditya is not a bad person. He has been deeply hurt, that's all. Give him time. Show him that he is safe with you; that he is secure.'

'I do not know what else I can do to make him see the love I have for him. But it is not about my love, Prats. It is about Antara's.'

'A child may be just the right antidote. I discouraged him earlier but perhaps it may give him the security he needs and bring the two of you closer.'

'We are trying, Prats. It is not as if I don't want to.' Her voice was immeasurably sad.

That evening, wine-sipping Tina tasted vodka for the first time in her young life. The solace she found in the hard-hitting liquor was a harbinger of the future.

18

Shaswati, their first born, brought with her toothless smile the possibility of happiness once again into Tina's life. The baby devoured all of Tina's time and energy, hungrily absorbed her mother's affections, and responded with devotion manifold. If she as much as sensed her mother's absence, she would create a ruckus until safely transported back to her mother's familiar, loving arms. Having the little one suckle at her breasts gave Tina indescribable joy. In motherhood she experienced a never-felt-before fulfilment. The child's tiny yet steady demands rejuvenated Tina's deflated passions and rekindled her smothered emotions.

In spite of her willingness, eighteen months had passed since their marriage before she had become pregnant. Aditya's relentless sniping had stopped with the confirmation of the pregnancy. During this period he had mellowed considerably but it had been evident to Tina that his concern was more for the unborn child than for Tina herself. From the beginning of the pregnancy he had harped upon the need to stop working and the inadvisability of driving down to Mahabaleshwar. In her seventh month Tina had finally given in.

With Shaswati's birth everything else faded into insignificance for Tina. The world of right angles and requisite light at Sanghavi's, of Manas and his tales of Gayatri, of weekends at Mahabaleshwar with Aditya's friends and Prats, became rarely thought-of memories in a distant past. She evinced no interest in resuming her Mahabaleshwar trips for work on the villa. Aditya had neither the time nor the inclination to oversee the renovation work; it remained at a standstill.

A few weeks after the birth she resumed her twice a week Kathak classes. During the twelve months that she had stayed away from Kathak, Poorvi too had become a mother. Shared motherhood brought the two friends closer. They deliberated over baby strollers whilst the others in the dance class – all society ladies – discussed the latest Mercedes models; compared notes on apple stew instead of Borsheim cheese recipes, baby powder instead of Shiseido cosmetics. Tina's afternoons or evenings were now spent with Poorvi and the two babies in the parks or at the paediatrician's.

As Shaswati took over Tina's universe Aditya was confined to its periphery, a situation not at all displeasing to him. His career, too, was waxing high.

'I have turned into the MD's right hand man, Prats. He trusts me more than the President. Maybe another year or two at most...'

'That was bound to happen. But right now I am more interested in Shaswati. Tell me about her?'

'Oh, she is an absolute darling! She has learnt to roll over by herself. We cannot leave her on the bed unattended for a minute.'

'Aah! My little sweetheart! It maddens me that I can't see her. This assignment will keep me in London for at least another month. Email me her pictures, Aditya. How is Tina?'

'Will pass on the line to her, Prats. Need to rush off to office. Bye!'

'Hello Prats! Long time!'

'Hi, beautiful! Yes, I have been missing all three of you, too. Tell me, how is our momma doing? Have you rejoined Sanghavi's?'

'Momma has time for nothing anymore, Shashy makes sure of that! I am not planning to rejoin work for a while now, Prats. Not that I mind at all!'

'Good! The baby needs you. How is Aditya?'

'He dotes on her, though his work leaves him with little time for her.' The earlier enthusiasm had left her voice.

'Are you happy, Tina?'

'Yes, Prats, everything is as it should be.'

'I am glad. Tell me more about her.'

'You know, Prats, conceiving her may have been the cause of our arguments but now, after her birth, it's easy to talk with Shashy between us.'

'Hmm.'

'I do not feel 'incomplete' anymore, Prats. Shashy completes me'.

'Yes. And perhaps parenthood will also 'complete' Aditya. He always wanted children. You will see, Tina, he will now treasure you, too. I'm happy things are going so well between the two of you.'

'Yes, they are.' Even as she concurred with Prashant no smile adorned her face, there was no light in her eyes. 'Come back soon, Prats. I have to go now, Shashy is squealing.'

The conversation with Prashant had left her restless. She ignored the squeals coming from the bathroom and headed straight to her room, locking the door behind her. She began writing in her diary. It had been months since the previous entry.

Everything is heading in the right direction? Is it normal not to make love for a month at an end? Am I that unsatisfying in bed? "Shaswati will wake up", he said again last night. It is always me who initiates; when he does, it is only lust. Over in minutes.

Was is it like this even at the beginning?

Everything for him is a well-chalked-out plan. Nothing because it simply 'is'.

There was a knock on the door. Even before the maid's voice came through the closed door, Shashy's hunger brawl made her breasts flow on their own. Tina quickly shut her diary and rushed towards the door.

She took the baby to her breast. With its flow, her tears ran too. Deep contentment now replaced the searing pain she had felt just a minute back. Tina could discern no clear source for the tears, neither in her mind nor her heart.

After feeding Shaswati she went back to her diary. Her thoughts were breaking down over each other. It had been a long time since she had allowed herself free expression, given free rein to her thoughts. A long while since the urge to write had overwhelmed her.

Happiness and sorrow in the end serve the same purpose.

I feel a heightened sense of awareness. I feel alive to the slightest of sensations. I feel like I'm responding to them from my deepest core.

Precious moments.

The entire universe lies open and unguarded for me to experience and know.

In the end everything is a part of one huge whole. My child, the sky outside my window, the air around me, the flower in the vase, the fire that burns in the kitchen, this fly buzzing in my room . . . all follow their own agenda, apparently disconnected, but very much like the neutrons, protons and electrons of an atom, irrevocably linked to each other, completing each other.

How can one erect a wall between parts of the same whole!

Our attempts at creating barriers only succeed in disturbing the free flow of life.

In the natural scheme of things, before the grandeur of nature, Aditya's obduracy is such a diminutive thing. . . .

Life is such a beautiful thing. . . .

A child is living proof of the highest joy possible between man and woman.

19

They were relaxing at home. Aditya and Tina sat by the windowsill, he trying to read a newsmagazine, and Tina just looking out over the ocean. Shashy, as they fondly called Shaswati, sat sucking a thumb in her rocker at their feet.

Aditya found the article a mere rehash of well-known facts. Bored with it, he let the magazine fall from his fingers and started examining the view from the window. His eyes fell upon a fishing boat. A man sat at the rudder and sitting quietly by him was a woman. They seemed to be returning home. The scene kindled memories of an earlier evening.

Aditya gently pulled Tina to him – something he had not done for a long time -- and held her tenderly in his arms.

Neither said a word. Each was lost in thought.

Tina, I am happy enough with this . . . as close to perfect as can be. . . .

Oh, Aditya! There is so much that we can be to each other. . . .

The boat had disappeared from view. The crimson sun set behind the ocean, painting the evening sky in myriad hues.

Perhaps Tamanna, who quickly followed Shaswati, was conceived that night.

20

Shortly after their fifth wedding anniversary – which they celebrated with a party at home for their friends – Aditya was appointed President of Soft Solutions. It was well received by the financial media. Occupying this august position in a professionally-run company at the age of 36 was considered a rare phenomenon. Aditya Malik was a man worth observing. Attached to the position was a luxurious sea-facing penthouse apartment in Colaba.

I have everything I ever desired: power, position, money, lovely children. And a beautiful, doting, intelligent wife who can be whatever I want her to be. . . .

Tina dutifully served her assigned role in Aditya's life. She played the part of the President's wife with dignity and grace. She managed her household with competence; balanced her time perfectly between domestic needs and her interests, be it work (she rejoined Sanghavi's part-time soon after Tamanna stopped feeding at her breast), her Kathak classes, or socialising. In bed, she was willing and satisfying. *Though perhaps not as enterprising and inventive as Antara. . . .*

There were moments when Aditya felt a little guilty about his manipulations of Tina. He assuaged his guilt in ways he found convenient. At these times, if Tina happened to express an interest in something that could be bought he would immediately buy it for her, or – as happened more often – he would give her the money and insist she purchase it. To himself, he would reason that it was a give and take world; he had provided her with all the comforts money could buy; he made no demands on her day; he had allowed her to continue her working relationship with that turd, Manas; and, of course, he did not cheat on her.

Not yet forty, with peppered hairdo, suave and agreeable manners, in a position of power and patronage, he was the boss everyone sought to please. Ambitious women seeking an easy climb up the corporate ladder, bored socialites, the naturally promiscuous – all pursued Aditya. Even though quite tempted at times, Aditya was conscious of the adherent risks to his blossoming career, and remained immune to all allurements. *She has been fair to me, and so must I be. . . .*

What of Tina? After her surrender to Aditya, she became adept at wearing her chosen mask of the perfect wife, hiding her innermost thoughts with increasing ingenuity. So successful she had become in subjugating her inner voice that it rarely asserted itself. When it did, she would call Prats and he always succeeded in bringing her round. If Prats happened to be unavailable she would seek an outlet in her diary. When it happened to assert itself all of a sudden, with Aditya as the cause, the mask would drop momentarily and there would be tiffs. But the mask would soon be back in place and she'd make her peace with him.

Aditya, when he sensed such bothersome 'intense' and 'passionate' moods in her, preferred to avoid her altogether: Aditya detested the intimate discussions she craved at such times. Outstation trips, board meetings, official evening dinners, extended golfing – there was no dearth of excuses to keep him away. They conveniently kept him busy till Tina had worked out her 'extreme emotions' and became 'pleasant and non-complicated' once again.

Once, when Tina had just finished reading Leo Tolstoy's *Anna Karenina*, she had recounted the tale in brief and pleaded with Aditya: 'I'm wasting myself away, Aditya. Tell me it is not so!' Immersing his head into some papers Aditya had muttered. 'It's just a book, Tina.'

Another time, a stray dog ran under her car wheels. Tina's remorse pangs lasted a week. His casual 'happens with strays' did nothing to console her. Aditya flew to Singapore on a business trip. As expected, by the time he returned, she had got over the incident.

When Upasna revealed her horror stories of wife-beating, Tina remained obsessed with the matter for weeks. Initially the tales of an abusive husband and the psychological roots of domestic violence piqued Aditya's interest but he soon got bored of it. During this period, Tina made frequent trips to Delhi to draw out her cousin from her 'depressive' and 'battered' state. Aditya was quite happy about it. *Better she deplete her energy sorting out her friend's causes than bother me with hers. . . .*

Tina's chatter about Poorvi and her high-brow tastes, or about Kriya and her 'all is fair in war attitude', Aditya found quaint and harmlessly refreshing.

To a silent Prats, Aditya once confided, 'Tina has a tendency for extreme emotions – anger, hatred, love, pity, etc. As long as they are not directed at me, I am okay with them. Generally she is pliable, accommodating and non-demanding. Of course, I can accept the occasional outburst of emotion. . .'

So, all in all, Aditya and Tina made a relative success of their marriage the first few years after the birth of Shaswati, their first-born.

Soon after Tamanna turned two, Tina started working full-time. With her creativity and adaptability, her proficiency in dealing with clients and co-workers, she had become a key player in Sanghvi's. Clients increasingly asked for her by name, wanting her to lead their assignments.

Shaswati had celebrated her sixth birthday, and Tamanna's fifth birthday was due in two months, when Aditya and Tina had their first major fight in a long, long time.

21

It began innocuously enough. They were invited to the fortieth wedding anniversary celebrations of the Chairman of Soft Solutions. Tina was busy with a crucial assignment at Sanghavi's. She called up Aditya and suggested he go alone to the party. He declined to do so, said the Chairman had specifically asked about Tina and he had confirmed that they both would be attending.

'Tell him I'm indisposed, Aditya. It's just a party and I have this important assignment to complete. It's a commitment. No one else can do it.'

Aditya had got angry. 'Resign if you have to. It is important to me that my wife be there with me.'

Tina reluctantly delegated the work to an assistant and left for home, quite upset herself at Aditya's typically selfish rejoinder. As they dressed for the party Aditya and Tina exchanged not a word. In the car, driving to the JW Marriott Hotel in Juhu where the party was being held, Aditya concentrated on his driving while Tina looked out the car window at the rain pelting down with monsoon fury on the gloom-enveloped city.

At the party they went their separate ways. Aditya joined his cronies and Tina chatted with the wives. She was bored to the hilt with the evening and soon she was on her third glass of wine whereas usually she restricted herself to a single glass. She resisted the urge to switch to vodka.

The famous ghazal singer Maan Singh took the stage. 'Life is about being in love,' he declaimed and requested the guests to take their seats with their wives or consorts. Tina looked around for Aditya and spotted him at the bar. To her uplifted eyes in query he shook his head and turned away.

In between two ghazals, as Maan Singh sipped some water, and there was relative silence in the vast lavishly appointed ballroom, Aditya heard the Chairman exclaim in his usual loud voice, 'You look ravishing today. But you always do! Without a doubt you are the most beautiful lady here tonight.'

The Chairman, non-executive head of Soft Solutions by dint of his influence with politicians and bureaucrats, was sitting with his wife to one side and Tina at the other. He was speaking to Tina, who was smiling. The Chairman's long-suffering wife caught Aditya's eye; to him it seemed she grimaced with embarrassment: her husband was known to be a notorious womaniser. Looking around, Aditya observed the smirks of amusement on the faces of his colleagues.

He felt humiliated. *Get up, Tina! Do not make a fool of me or of yourself!*

Tina remained seated. During the next ghazal Aditya's eyes stayed glued on them. The Chairman would lean towards Tina and say something; Tina would smile and murmur back. To Aditya it seemed she was enjoying the attention. He replenished his drink. Turning from the bar he saw Tina looking directly at him. Her eyes

and expression suggested she were asking him something. He cut
her gaze and began chatting with an acquaintance.

'Aditya, should we eat? Hello, Mr Bakshi.' She had made her
way to them.

'Hello, Tina,' returned Mr Bakshi.

'You have your dinner. I will be having another drink.' Aditya's
tone was polite but he knew Tina understood.

'Okay.'

For the rest of the evening Aditya contrived to ensure Tina
never got an opportunity to find him alone. They finally left the
party after midnight. Both had consumed copious amounts of
alcohol. Neither had eaten much.

Waiting on the hotel steps for their car to be brought round,
Tina felt soothed by the cool monsoon breeze. The rain had
stopped.

Once in the car, Tina tried to discuss the evening.

'Maan Singh was very good. I thought he sang *Pyar bhar*
extremely well.'

'Sethna's have shifted their kids to Cathedral.'

'The ravioli could have been creamier, don't you think?'

Aditya answered in monologues. Eventually she asked him,
'What's wrong?'

'Nothing.' His tone was flat.

'Of course it's not nothing! What is it, tell me?'

'I need to spell it out for you? Every single person in the party
noticed!' His voice oozed venom.

'Aah! So it is about me sitting next to your flirting Chairman.
Aditya, are you jealous?' Tina's voice became teasing. 'Mmm . . . so
Mr Aditya Malik feels jealous, too. . .' She chewed her lower lip.

If Tina could have seen Aditya's eyes she would have turned to
ashes.

'Jealous! I am not jealous! I am disgraced! I feel fucking insulted, a fool. And you, my so-called smart, adoring, intelligent wife – who so shamelessly pandered to that old fart's flirting tricks – thinks I am jealous? You think he was interested in you? He was just amusing himself for the evening and you allowed yourself to become his toy. What kind of a fool have I married?'

'Aditya, you're making a big deal out of nothing. I was trying to be nice to him, nothing else. After all he is your boss, isn't he?'

'I do not need to pimp my wife to ensure my position in the company. Do not dare to use that excuse with me. You relished the attention you got. I could see that.'

'Aditya! What a thing to say! And you don't need to shout like this! I forego my commitments for the sake of yours and this is what I get in return! You had said it was important your wife be with you this evening, yet you ignored me the whole evening. Almost everybody was sitting as a couple. I was looking for you when the Chairman noticed and made me sit by him. You could have fetched me from there, yet you made no effort to do so. At least he was nice to me.'

'Oh, women! Pay them a little attention and they will do anything to feel important. First that dithering Manas, now this doddering geriatric!'

'You make me sound like a whore! Go to hell! I don't need to deal with this. I've had enough of you!'

'No, I have had enough of you, Tina.'

'How could you have had enough of me, Aditya? You haven't even given me a decent chance. You never stopped loving her for a moment.'

There was silence in the car. As Tina bit her lip, Aditya spoke. His voice was stone cold.

'Yes, I still love her. So, are you going to ask me for a divorce, Tina? What are you going to do about it?'

'Then go to her! Why are you here with me?' Tina's eyes clouded with tears.

'I will do what I want to. I do not need your permission.'

Aditya manoeuvred the car to the kerb and switched off the ignition. He got out, walked a few paces ahead, and lit a cigarette. He didn't notice that a silver Honda had also stopped some yards behind his car. Its driver was in shadow.

Tina stayed rooted to her seat. She observed the rain-washed moonlit outline of Haji Ali with unseeing eyes.

I wish my friends were here. Kriya's in Pune, Poorvi in Delhi, Upasna abroad, and now Manas has run off in pursuit of Gayatri to Chennai.

Her mouth was dry; she felt thirsty, and impatient to be home. There, a bottle of Smirnoff awaited her.

When Aditya got in, neither spoke. He dropped her home and drove away. He hadn't noticed the silver Honda that had followed them from the Marriott, had stopped well behind his vehicle at Haji Ali, now parked outside his building complex.

After he drove away its lone occupant stepped down and stood gazing at the twin-winged building. A window sprang to life in the dark hall of the building, on the uppermost floor of one of the wings.

She smiled.

She had kept herself well-hidden at the party. Yet she had closely observed the couple, particularly Aditya.

That old Henry was getting on my nerves. Sex maniac!

She inhaled deeply as the salt wafted through her nostrils.

22

'Can I call you back, Prats? I am in a meeting.' Aditya said over the phone the next afternoon.

'No. We need to speak right now. It is important.' Prashant sounded perturbed.

'Okay. Hold on a moment . . . Sorry, people, I have to take this call. Please continue. I will be back shortly.'

Once out of the conference room, he told Prashant to go ahead.

'What happened between the two of you?'

'Prats, I thought you said it was urgent. I was in the middle of a meeting!'

'Tina is here, in Mahabaleshwar.'

'What shit! We had a small argument yesterday. Why cannot she behave more maturely? She is a mother of two for heaven's sake. Prats, tell her to start back this instant. I don't care if she has to drive through the dark.' Aditya swore under his breath.

'She is not in her senses, Aditya. She has finished an entire bottle of vodka!'

23

Thereafter, their relationship deteriorated; whatever warmth there had been between them, vanished. Their manner towards each other, at the best of times, became cool and indifferent; at the worst of times neither Aditya nor Tina let an opportunity pass to needle the other, each quick to respond with sharpness. Irritations no longer remained internalised, were manifested promptly. Minor disagreements often snowballed into major arguments. Their restraint lasted only as long as they were within earshot, or sight, of others.

With some friends they were watching Deepa Mehta's *Water* in a theatre. Tina was deeply moved by the child widow's plight. In the closing scenes, at the sight of the little girl's blood-stained white saree, she started sobbing audibly. Aditya noticed heads turn and look in their direction. He elbowed Tina. To no avail. Tina was still sniffing as they shuffled out of the theatre, drawing glances from other theatre-goers. Aditya overheard a woman whispering to her companion, 'God knows what that woman is going through.'

Their friends dropped them off and, the moment they were alone, Aditya gave vent to his irritation.

'I know it was a sensitive movie, but must you make a spectacle of yourself! You were the only one in the entire theatre snivelling so loudly. Why the hell cannot you be like others? Must you always wear your feelings on your sleeve?'

'The movie bored you, didn't it? You were fidgeting in your seat the entire time. Don't insult other people's emotions and feelings,' Tina retorted.

'Emotions! Feelings! Love! I am sick of it! You and your extravagant passions are driving me up the wall.'

'You, Mr Cool, have no feelings! Not any more . . . don't tell me how to handle mine. In any case they are not directed at you.'

'Yes, I can no longer feel anything for anyone, least of all for you! I spent all my feelings on Antara. Is that what you want to hear?'

'No, Aditya, I don't. But it has become the goddamn reality of my life! Why did you come to the gallery that evening at all, Aditya? Why did you choose to come into my life?'

'I wanted a wife and children. You fitted my requirements well. That is why I came.'

'I fitted your requirements well! Was I a vase, or a trifling piece of furniture, you desired for your living room? A lifeless trophy to be shown-off?'

Aditya busied himself at his wardrobe.

Tina was sitting at her dressing table. She spoke after a long pause. The fire had gone out of her voice. It was soft, introspective.

'This can't be true! Ten years of togetherness, two children, and a life that is woven around you . . . only to be told that I just fitted-in well . . . Have you never really cared for me, Aditya? Never loved me? Even for a while? I need to know, Aditya. Please tell me!'

'You want the truth? Here it is . . . What is most 'you' is odious to me. Your 'love' belittles you, makes you desperate. Your incessant hope, the lost self-pride . . . Oh, Tina, I hate it all and I hate you for it!'

Tina's reply was a whisper, as if she were really addressing her reflection in the mirror, rather than speaking to Aditya. There was a deep angst in it.

'What am I doing here, then? In this house . . . your house?'

For a few moments Aditya stood stock still. Then he took his wallet from the wardrobe and put it back in his pocket. Without a word he left the room and walked out of the penthouse.

Tina stood frozen at her dressing table, staring into the mirror.

'He hates me.'

'What am I doing here?'

'Why am I here?'

No matter how she posed the questions, how she phrased her tumultuous thoughts, her reflection merely mouthed them back. It would not say the words she had racing inside her head: 'Leave him.'

In the end, vodka shots made the question less compelling.

The door to her room remained locked. In the children's bedroom Kantabai, their maid, hugged the girls close and fell asleep with them on their bed.

Down below, in the third floor apartment of the adjacent wing, Antara lounged in a deep leather sofa, sipping Carenum in a crystal wineglass. She raised a toast to the absent Henry – he had gifted to her a case of the rare, exotic French wine. Inserting a videocassette into the player she had just acquired – with some difficulty as VCRs had become relics of another generation – she nibbled a cube of Parmigiano cheese.

Adi is still as handsome . . . better, in fact . . . he has aged well. . . .

24

Antara, was an air hostess with Indian Airlines when she had fallen into Aditya's lap. Her beat at the time was Bangalore-Bombay-Bangalore. The aircraft had hit an air pocket just as she was walking down the aisle. She stumbled and fell into the lap of the occupant of an aisle seat.

The startled man had beamed at her and said, 'Hello, angel!'

'Hi! I'm sorry, sir!' mumbled the flustered Antara as she scrambled up.

'No harm done.'

The fleeting glimpse she had of the man stayed with her as she continued down the aisle. He was young and handsome, and well-dressed. She smiled to herself. A few minutes later she was in the galley preparing the food trolley when she looked up to see him grinning at her.

There is a smouldering intensity in her gaze. Men have drowned in them, and she knows it.

'You are the most beautiful woman to have sat on my lap. Are you from Bangalore, Antara?' Her name was imprinted on the name tag she wore on her chest. She laughed.

Mmmm . . . he has promise.

They started chatting.

Aditya was travelling from Bombay to Bangalore to take up his first job with an MNC there. He had recently passed out of IIM, Ahmedabad, where he had been recruited in a campus interview, and had been visiting his uncle in Mahabaleshwar. It would be his first time in Bangalore. He knew nobody in the city.

Antara was based in Bangalore. She offered to familiarise him with the city. Her offer was readily accepted.

So Aditya and Antara became good friends. Speaking to a woman friend she confided that not only was he tall, handsome and always well-dressed, he was intelligent, witty and quite urbane. He had been a topper at IIM and many companies had competed to recruit him. The package offered by the Bangalore-based MNC had set a new record. Her friend suggested Antara dump her regular boyfriend and ensure this 'prize catch' didn't get away.

'Hey, steady-on, girl! I'm not ready for the marriage shit just yet. Before I settle down I want to travel, see the world, experience things . . .'

Aditya had fallen in love with Antara. As an undergraduate in Sydenham he had been pursued by many girls; even in IIM Ahmedabad, despite the skewed boy-girl ratio and the impressive choice available to them, Aditya had melted many a female heart. But till Antara came along, Aditya had himself never chased a girl, nor allowed any to become a regular girlfriend; for him they had been companions of an evening or a night, nothing more. His energies were predominantly directed at ensuring a good start to his corporate career.

The good start that he had aimed for was in fact a resounding beginning. Now he was ready to think about his secondary needs. His parents had died in a car crash when he had been just seven years old. The only family he had was Prashant, his mother's younger brother. He wanted his own family: a wife, and children.

Within days of their first meeting Aditya and Antara became lovers.

Antara, besides being a beautiful and confident young woman, was a natural extrovert, an excellent conversationalist, and very well-informed. She could hold her own in any conversation. Physically, Aditya found her dusky complexion and flawless skin very attractive. In bed she was a veritable tigress. She had no inhibitions and her proclivity for adventure and experimentation introduced Aditya to pleasures he had never imagined possible. Sex had never satisfied him more. In fact, in all his short liaisons, his sexual appetite had been soon sated, and been followed by a complete loss of interest in the girl of the moment. With Antara he craved more, and yet more. . . .

'Do you know what day it is today, Antz?'

'Thursday. Why?'

'I am not referring to the day of the week! Today is the fiftieth day after our first meeting, Antz. When you fell into my lap. . .'

As he spoke, Aditya fished out a small box from his pocket and handed it to her. Laughing, Antara unwrapped the small parcel. She opened it and her eyes widened at seeing the diamond ring sitting in its soft satin bed.

'Marry me, Antz.'

Antara smiled and looked at him quizzically. Aditya noticed her eyes flitting between him and the diamond ring, with which she was fidgeting. A few moments passed in silence. When she spoke, it was in a soft pensive voice. 'I need to think about it, Adi.'

She is not as madly in love with me as I with her. She likes me well enough, though. But she will be mine, exclusively mine. . . .

A month thereafter they were married in Bangalore. Prashant was present. He was not too pleased with his erstwhile ward's decision, but knew him well enough to keep his doubts to himself.

Aditya had accumulated only enough leave to allow them an extended weekend honeymoon so they went to nearby Coonoor. It was a particularly wet weekend but that mattered not a whit to the young couple. They were happy to remain in their bedroom.

In all his previous relationships, women had surrendered themselves to him. Had he wanted to, he could have dictated their mind, body and soul. None had interested him enough to want to do so. Antara gave him unreserved access to her body while keeping her core aloof. Their marital life was easy and full of fun; but there were moments when, though physically with him, he sensed her mind far away, in a place that remained impenetrable to him. Try as he might she would not share these private thoughts, not even provide the merest glimpse. Aditya was puzzled by this secret side otherwise so-open self, but not unduly perturbed. In fact the mystery added spice to their relationship. Aditya loved challenges. All his life he had welcomed them. So for him it was more of a challenge to get her to expose these innermost thoughts. Aditya worked assiduously at it. He was a loving, caring husband, showering her with little gifts and fulfilling her merest desires.

I will possess her completely. It is only a matter of time and patience.

The months passed. Antara switched jobs while still remaining an air hostess. She joined an international airline that had begun flights to Bangalore, which meant her absences were of a longer duration. Aditya was busy making himself indispensable to the company he worked for, so he did not mind. Whenever she returned from a trip they were hungry for each other. Lying in bed after a bout of sex she would regale him with tidbits from her trip. Aditya loved her stories and looked forward to them almost as much as he hankered for her body.

Aditya was happy. Just before their first wedding anniversary he admitted to Prashant, in one of their regular telephone conversations, that he had never been happier in his life.

Where and how to celebrate their first anniversary was their first minor quibble. He wanted it to be in Mahabaleshwar as he had been unable to visit Prashant since coming to Bangalore. She wanted to go to Mauritius. They settled on Goa.

Their second minor quibble occurred the night after their first wedding anniversary. It was their last night in Goa and they were lying in bed after making love. Aditya expressed the desire to start a family. Antara laughed and told him not to be ridiculous. When he persisted and tried reasoning with her she told him in exasperation that she would think about it. To pre-empt any further discussion of the vexing issue Antara began to fondle Aditya in a way she knew was bound to arouse him.

Back in Bangalore Aditya tried often, always without success, to get Antara to discuss the matter. One evening, after Aditya would not allow her to toss-off the subject lightly, as she had been doing now for months, Antara showed irritation for the first time in their short married life.

'But a child at this point would mean giving up my job, Adi. You know I can't do that!'

'You cannot or you do not want to?'

She flinched at his sharpness. With matching alacrity she retorted, 'Does it matter? We had spoken about this kid business at the time of our wedding. We had agreed that neither of us wanted kids soon. So why are you going back on your words?'

Aditya's voice softened as he reasoned with her.

'But that was then, Antara. We have been married nearly two years. Priorities change. Desires evolve. I feel safe in my job. My career is going well. I feel the time has come to start a family. Be reasonable, Antz.'

'Well, I will explain why I am so averse to the idea. Having a child may just be a matter of convenience for you; it doesn't make the same demands on you as it would on me. The woman's inconvenience is something that completely evades the sensibility of you men! You can go about your life unhindered; it is I who will have to give up everything I have worked hard for. You know I'm being considered for the first class cabin, something that I've been striving for all along. I become pregnant and . . . forget the first class, I'll be grounded and be assigned a boring desk job. Do you have any idea at all what it would mean for me! A year in the first class section, and every single major airline would flood me with better offers! Why would I want to throw it all up? What for? To look fat and ugly? Soon you, too, will find me undesirable. I have seen many colleagues fall for it... this family business. I am certainly not one of them.

'For you to even propose having children at this juncture, and not think of its adverse ramifications for me, only shows how typical an Indian male you are. All your declarations of being liberal are a sham!'

Aditya had been listening to her in stunned silence. When he spoke, the softness remained but it was tinged with bitterness.

'I never considered you as being separate from myself, Antz! Which woman would not want to be a mother? Procreation is not something distasteful, it is pure joy. And it is not as if your life will end, you can go back to your job within a year or two. I cannot believe you can be so selfish about it... this selfishness over something so fundamental to being human, to marriage!'

'Adi, I had no plans to get married for a long time when you came along with your proposal. If you remember I told you I needed time to think. It is you who pestered me into it. It was for this very reason I was reluctant. Now don't give me this crap on womanhood and motherhood, please. It stinks. I never claimed to be the '*adarsh bharatiya nari*', nor am I going to allow you to emotionally blackmail me. It is downright deplorable of you to attack me the way you just did.'

'I'm sorry you feel like this, Antz. Let's discuss this later.'

Antara never initiated discussion on the subject. Whenever Aditya tried to do so, her stock rejoinder was a brief 'No'.

They continued as before but with cooler spirits. A chasm had opened up between them that, even as it stayed narrow, remained deep. Their fun evenings no longer had the same gaiety. Their erotic explorations became awkward. More and more often sex became just the mere act of copulation, of the swift satisfaction of physical needs. The magic had gone out of the relationship.

The second anniversary of their marriage was approaching. One evening Aditya tentatively proposed a week in Mauritius.

'Aditya, we need to sit and talk.'

Her boss and she had developed a relationship. He was transferring to the UK and had asked her to join him. She had agreed.

'I'm going with him, Aditya.'

'What do you mean, you are going with him?' Aditya was shell-shocked.

'Our marriage is over, Aditya. I see no reason why we should maintain this farce.'

'Yes, we have had major differences, but that does not mean that the marriage is over. For Christ's sake, don't you love me anymore? I do. I have never loved you a speck less all through these days.'

'There is no point in going into all of that now, Adi. It is too late. I want a divorce, but whether I get it or not, I am still leaving with him.'

He sensed the finality in her voice. 'But he is married, with two kids, isn't he?' blurted Aditya, clutching at straws, the panic in his voice barely restrained.

'Yes, he is. But she has agreed to a divorce. He made her an offer she couldn't refuse. You see, he can make one. He has the money.' The glint in her eyes made him squirm. She knew of his weak spot. Aditya quietly left the room.

A few days later Antara left for the UK Aditya received the divorce papers in the mail soon thereafter. He signed and posted them back to her London address, of which he made no note.

Upon Antara's departure Aditya started applying for a new job. His preference was for Bombay. With his impeccable work credentials and brilliant academic record he received several offers. Those from Bangalore·or anywhere in the south he rejected out of hand. He finally chose Soft Solutions, a dynamic up-coming company operating out of Bombay. When he moved from Bangalore he left with just two suitcases. The entire contents of the Bangalore flat were sold off at whatever prices they could fetch. He did not even retain a photograph of Antara.

25

Antara was having a massage. She grimaced as the masseur pressed a nerve in her thigh. Used as she was to the finest spas of Europe she had found the stout middle-aged woman to be a poorly trained exponent of the art of massage. The uneducated woman had little knowledge of the human anatomy, knew nothing of its intricate working. Her hands were rough and she was tardy in trimming her nails. Before beginning a massage, Antara always insisted the woman wash her hands thoroughly with soap and water, later discarding the used towel with the tips of her fingers in a small bin she kept specifically for the purpose (her maid was instructed to wash it separately from Antara's own soiled clothes). But Antara had not retained the woman for her ability to give a satisfactory massage. Initially that had been the reason but Antara had been quick to realise that in the garrulous woman she had a valuable source of information.

The woman, having worked in the area for years, knew most of the menials working in the apartments. Over the years she had built up an impressive network of sources for the gossip that was as much her stock-in-trade as her massages. With native cleverness she had discerned Antara's specific interest in Tina, another occupant of the same building.

'Tina madam has had another fight with her man. Another *bilayati* bottle emptied. Kantabai, her maid, has become a regular supplier of them to the *raddiwallah*. They screamed at each other so loud that Premabai two floors down could hear them. It has become an almost daily feature. They fight. He storms out of the house. And Madam picks up her bottle. She drinks like a fish. A bottle in her hand has to be emptied. The liquor shop owner at the corner says his sales to the household have seen a huge jump. He's had to increase his order of supply for the *bilayati maal*. . . .'

After the woman had left, relaxing in her warm bath, sipping her wine (she had switched to plainer stuff as Henry's gift had run out), Antara ruminated over the matter that had exercised her exclusive interest these past weeks in Mumbai.

They are doing fabulously well! Without my help, too! I think I can safely leave them to it while I make a trip to London. I need fresh lingerie. And Henry can replenish my cellar.

It's time to settle accounts with him. He thinks I don't know about his little slut, the old fart! Let us see how much she is worth . . . Divorce time, Henry!

The next day Antara flew to London, telling her maid she would be back soon.

26

Soon after her Mahabaleshwar binge Tina resigned from Sanghavi's. Her public explanation: 'increasing family obligations', 'the kids are growing up, I need to give more time to them.' Aditya shrugged off her decision. Prashant was upset about it but, faced with Aditya's indifference and Tina's own growing aloofness, found he couldn't do a thing about it.

After the *Water* episode she became irregular in her visits to Anarth. Outings with friends became rarer. She no longer took the initiative to make programmes and if they called she pleaded a headache, children's needs, or just that she wasn't in the mood. Only when a friend like Poorvi badgered her did she venture out of the house.

Upasna called. She was over on a flying visit from Delhi. Sensing her cousin's mood she tried to probe further but Tina shut her out; saying she had to go Tina cut the connection. Upasna redialled but Tina did not answer.

Manas telephoned. He was back from Chennai. She expressed pleasure at his return, commiserated with him over Gayatri. Even though her responses were 'correct' Manas knew Tina too well not to detect that something was amiss. He asked her what the matter was. 'Nothing,' she replied. He persisted with his questions, receiving cryptic monosyllabic replies. He was as unsuccessful as Upasna.

Kriya telephoned. She would not be brushed away as easily as Upasna and Manas had been. Tina told her 'problems with Aditya'. Kriya insisted on learning more. Tina told her a little. Kriya was smart enough to read between the lines. Drawing her own inferences she told her friend bluntly: leave him. She had added, 'You are strong enough to stand on your own two feet Tina.' If Kriya could have seen her friend she would have seen a look of utter hopelessness in her eyes.

Prashant passed through Mumbai on his way abroad for an assignment. He spent a few hours with them at home and went away a disturbed man.

Tina tagged along with Aditya and the kids on family outings but with little enthusiasm. If Aditya was firm enough she accompanied him to parties and official or social functions.

She increasingly left the household and the children to manage themselves.

The first weeks after the *Water* episode they had frequent arguments. They had stopped bothering about the kids overhearing, often they quarrelled in their presence. Either one or the other would end up sleeping in the guest room.

Tina began drinking heavily. Most days she worked her way steadily through a bottle of vodka. She took to napping in the afternoons, something she had rarely indulged in earlier. Aditya lengthened his work-day and rarely returned home earlier than dinnertime; by then Tina would be in a stupor and be least interested in conversation of any sort. When they ventured out as a family Tina would be, more often than not, lost in her own soporific world. Aditya would entertain the children and converse with them.

As Tina's alcoholic bouts increased, their frequency of quarrelling declined. At times, sensing an argument shaping-up, she would withdraw into herself, allow Aditya to have his say. Other times their arguments would reverberate through the apartment. Frequency may have declined, but the intensity had increased.

One evening, days after Antara had left for London, Tina collapsed in the bathroom. Shaswati and Tamanna witnessed their mother being carted off on a stretcher. The stink of vomit could not be hidden by the white sheets that covered her frail body. Her state of delirium was all too evident and scared the kids, particularly five-year-old Tamanna. Aditya packed them off to Tina's parents in Kolkata. A week later, when it was time for them to return, Tamanna told her *nani* she didn't want to go back. 'Mommy scares me,' she mumbled through her sobs. Aditya had to cajole her on the telephone into agreeing to return. Shaswati took the phone from her sibling and told Aditya, 'Daddy, please don't bring Mommy to pick us up from the airport. Come alone.'

In the car, Shaswati spoke with a maturity beyond her years. 'Mommy has begun to drink too much. Why, Daddy?'

Aditya remained silent.

'My friends at school look at me strangely, whispering things. They stop when I go near them. I can't hear them, but I know they are talking about Mommy and you. The other day, Ekta told me that her mom tells her not to be with me too much. I hate Ekta's mommy. I don't want to go to school at all, Daddy.'

Tamanna too piped up, her voice shaky. 'I don't want to go to school too. I don't want to go to Mommy either. I don't like her any more.'

'But why is Mommy drinking so much of that horrible stuff, Daddy? She never did before. . .' Shaswati's voice tapered off.

Aditya was shaken to the core. *Yes, why?*

'Daddy, I once heard mommy scream she would kill herself. Will she really leave us and go away? Will you then get another mommy for us? And will she be like Cinderella's step-mom? I asked *nani* but she started crying too,' Tamanna asked.

Shaswati looked him in the eye and said, 'Mommy has changed. And I know the two of you don't love each other. I heard you say so yourself, that you are together only because of us. You both hate each other, don't you?'

Tamanna: 'Did you change Mommy, Daddy?'

Aditya felt as if he had been struck. The child's innocent but true words hit him hard. His hands shook as he brushed away an imaginary fly from his face.

Yes, Tamanna, it is I who am to blame. I am sorry, my little darlings for what I have done to your mother, for what I have made the two of you go through. I am responsible for your pain, for your fear and insecurity.

He hugged the children close to himself.

Tina was right. I had no right to marry her, to bring you into this world. I have destroyed your mother. She has paid a high price for her love. Had she loved me less, she would not have been the wreck she is today.

And you, my darlings, too are paying the price. . . .

Oh, Antara! What have you done! I will not give you the satisfaction of destroying innocent others! I will end the cycle of destruction you have engineered.

Aditya lifted their chins and, looking both in the eye, said, 'Everything will be okay, I promise you. Mommy will be fine. I will ensure you have your old Mommy back.'

Aditya's raised eyebrows quizzed them, asking if they believed him. Shaswati nodded back and Tamanna imitated her elder sister, as she always did.

'Okay. Now how about McDonald's to cheer-up my two angels?'

Emphatic nods indicated their approval. Aditya instructed the driver to take them to the drive-through McDonald's. French fries, *aloo tikki* burger and chocolate milk shake, kept the children busy as they drove home.

Shaswati and Tamanna avoided Tina the whole day, sticking to their father or keeping to themselves. Tina followed them with her eyes where she could but made no attempt to accost them, not knowing how to apologise.

The family finally gathered at the dinner table and Aditya began his salvage operation.

'Shashy, Tamanna, Mommy is as upset as you two are. Give Mommy a hug.'

Tamanna was ready to fly into her mother's arms but stopped when she saw Shaswati still seated. She sank back into her chair.

Tina looked at them with puffy, sad eyes and said, 'I'm sorry for everything, but I love you two. More than I love myself. Can you give me a hug please. . . ?'

Shaswati rose gingerly. Tamanna instantly followed. The three clasped each other in a tight hug.

Once the dinner was over, Shaswati asked, 'Mommy, will you read *Hitler's Canary* to us?'

With their simplicity and readiness to forget, to start anew – as only children can – they once again placed their faith in Tina.

'Yes, I would love to. Let's go.' Tina's eyes sparkled for the first time in days.

Once they had fallen asleep, Tina sat by herself on the window sill, overlooking the dark ocean, nursing a cup of coffee. On her face was a look of utter dejection. Aditya joined her. For a few minutes neither spoke, each looking out of the window into the dark night. A gentle sea-breeze susurrated the curtains, unseen waves crashed on the shore below them.

'Tina, I want to make this marriage work.'

The merest flutter of her eyelids was the only indication that she had heard.

'Do you think we can start afresh, as much for the kids as for us? Let us put our past behind us.'

After a long pause, Tina replied, her monosyllabic reply barely audible.

'Yes.'

'The kids seem to be okay for now.'

For the first time she looked at him and spoke, 'Are they?'

'They are. The rest, a normal atmosphere will achieve. Tina, why not rejoin Sanghavi's? Or any other firm? The kids are away for most of the day.'

'Work?'

He nodded.

'Aditya, I don't have the focus that work requires. I . . . I can't even manage myself, how will I manage others. You know, I tell myself over and over again that I should not drink, yet I do. I can't help myself. I don't know what to do.'

Tina's voice was calm, matter-of-fact. It was as if she were talking about a distant friend and not herself.

The next day Aditya made some enquiries. He came home early and spent the entire evening with Tina. There was little conversation but neither felt the need for it, being content to watch television or listen to the children's prattle.

That night, as they lay side by side on the bed, Aditya tentatively broached the matter that had been on his mind the last twenty-four hours.

'Tina, do you want to go into rehab?'

'You think I should?'

'Yes, it will help.'

'Okay.'

The counsellor at the de-addiction centre prescribed an eight-week residential programme during which she was barred from communicating with family or the outside world. A single phone call was permitted at the end of the fourth week. She utilised it to speak with the children. Aditya, too, spoke to her. They wished each other for their tenth wedding anniversary.

Aditya was in a conference with his executives when his cellphone started flashing. It was an unknown number. Aditya assumed it must be a telemarketer and returned his attention to the ongoing discussion of business plans for the next quarter. A few minutes later he began fiddling with the instrument, looking repeatedly at the first item under missed calls. Something about the number disturbed him but he couldn't fathom the cause. He caught the quizzical look of a colleague.

'Something has come up. I regret we will have to conclude this meeting now. Thank you, people.'

As soon as he was alone Aditya dialled the strange number. *This is ridiculous!* Aditya reprimanded himself.

'I have a missed call from this number?' His tone was crisp and interrogative, with an undisguised tinge of irritation.

'Hello Aditya. This is I.' In a flash he understood why the number had disturbed him. Its last four digits were her favoured combination. The voice, though subdued, was unmistakable, confident, and seductive.

'Antara?'

'Yes, the girl who fell into your lap.'

'Ohmygod!'

Aditya always spoke with deliberation. His words never ran into each other. A thrill ran down his spine, his eyes lit up. Without thinking he used the love-name he had coined. 'How are you, Antz?'

'I am well, Adi. Couldn't be better . . . I hope I can call you 'Adi'?'

'Of course! Did I not just call you 'Antz'?'

The initial excitement was dissipating, harsh memories sparking. His mind was reasserting its usual control. *A 91 prefix . . . what's she doing here?*

'What brings you back to India, Antz? We have not kept up with each other for years, so why this call now?'

Disregarding his first query she answered his second, with a question of her own.

'Is that a complaint or a warning?'

Aditya visualised her sensuous lips curving. . . .

'What if it's a complaint?' he countered. It had been quite a while since he had played the cat and mouse game with a woman.

'Then I would say I'm glad to be back home,' she replied with unexpected seriousness.

'What happened, Antara? Where is that fellow . . . ? I can't remember his name.' There was clear impatience in his voice.

'You want me to pack ten years through this insignificant little mouthpiece, Adi? Let's meet for coffee, Mr President.' The teasing tone was back.

'You are in Mumbai? What are you doing here?'

'In good time, Adi. Over coffee. How about the Barista near your office? Tomorrow evening, seven, okay with you? Unless. . .' Antara allowed her voice to taper off.

As anticipated by Antara, Aditya was intrigued by her knowledge of him. It showed she had done some homework on him. *Why?*

Aditya noticed the blinking light on his complex desk phone. The MD of Soft Solutions was calling. He spoke abruptly into the cell phone.

'Seven it is. I have to go now, Antara.'

That little vixen!

Aditya entered Barista five minutes before the appointed hour. His eyes were immediately drawn to the lone woman occupying a table for four in a quiet corner. She was speaking into her cell. Through her slightly bent frame and maroon t-shirt -- with its deep neckline -- Aditya could see a rich tan that set her dusky skin aglow. As he made his way towards her his gaze fell on her long legs, gingerly crossed over each other, revealing well-toned calf muscles. *They would still be as vigorous -- that's Antara, all promise -- from toe to head.*

Antara looked up, saw him, and waved.

'Hello, gorgeous!' Aditya said, extending his arm for a handshake.

'Not like this, handsome.'

Antara pulled him in a tight hug. Aditya inhaled the familiar Ylang Ylang across her smooth nape.

'It's good to see you, Adi,' she murmured softly in his ears.

'It is good to see you too, Antara,' Aditya replied, though a little cautiously.

Antara examined him from head to toe.

'Rolex Oyster wristwatch, Feragamo shoes . . . nothing but the very best for you, Mr Aditya Malik -- just as you had promised!'

He looked meaningfully at the large diamond ring on her finger before retorting.

'You seem to have done well for yourself, too, Antara. What do I use as the family name, darling?'

'Just Antara is fine, Adi.' She smiled. Aditya marked the lack of warmth in the smile. *Cool bitch!*

They fenced around, each manoeuvring to retain control over the evening, each fully aware of their mutual endeavour to do so.

Aditya was the first to lose patience.

'I guess I have managed well enough all these years, in spite of your desertion. You gave me up as a lost cause, didn't you, darling!'

'Not for a second did I doubt that you would succeed. You were always destined to be on top. That was never the issue, Adi. Our problem was that I too was destined to be on top. For a marriage to succeed, only one can be.'

She paused before continuing, allowing the words to sink in.

'That's why I came back. . .'

'A lioness never surrenders, Antara.'

'A lioness, or a lion for that matter, first stalks its prey; then it's the thrill of the chase, and finally it's the catch. But after the kill, the lioness, even if the kill is hers, grants the lion first rights over the kill. It is not surrender. You see, even in the animal kingdom, there can be only one master . . . But let's not get into these morbid areas today, Adi. We're meeting after such a long time.

'The youngest President of Soft Solutions! Where to, from here, Adi?' she said, steering the conversation with practised flair.

Aditya had arrived for the meeting with two clear objectives. First, he wanted Antara to know what she had walked out on. He thought she had learnt the superficial details of his life from some source – not so difficult given his current status in Mumbai society – but he never for a moment imagined she would know as much as she did. She herself was careful not to reveal her full knowledge.

He spoke of his rapid climb up the corporate ladder, his marriage to the beautiful Tina; of his lovely children Shaswati and Tamanna; of the high life he led in Mumbai, his extensive travels within the country and abroad; he raved about his lavish penthouse in Mumbai, his sprawling weekend home in Mahabaleshwar. Antara, of course, knew all this and more; she listened to his versions with ostensibly keen interest, egging him on as and when she felt was necessary.

Aditya's other objective was to satisfy his great curiosity about her own life after she had left him. He knew nothing of it.

'But tell me about yourself, Antara. I can certainly see the signs of your success. Solitaire ring, Chanel t-shirt! I am sure that is a Bauget on your slim wrist. '

'All bought from *moi's* sweat and blood, Adi. For years I criss-crossed the world as an air hostess. First class all through, of course. I met the most interesting and powerful people – senior diplomats, senators and ministers, business magnates, executive honchos, Hollywood stars, rock stars, and so forth. Got proposed umpteen times by the who's who. . .'

She spoke in generalities. Whenever Aditya attempted to probe into her personal life she deftly sidestepped his queries and comments with tales of interesting or bizarre encounters, much as she had regaled him in Bangalore. She had always been a skilled conversationalist and story-teller. Now, Aditya soon realised, she was a consummate artist.

No Mumbai socialite, however urbane, could match her wit and panache. She had gained vast experience of the world. Her level of knowledge and understanding of world affairs was astonishing. She had observed people with astuteness, spoke of them with astounding perspicacity.

He relaxed and started enjoying the evening.

If she had been a liberated soul before, now she had crossed all boundaries. With her bold opinions on everything from coffee to infidelity she had Aditya in splits. No extramarital affair was unbelievable, threesome in sex was not perverse but people's way of dealing with boredom; the ones who didn't bitch were potentially less safe than the ones who did, for nothing was more natural than the desire to bitch.

'Men can come from as diverse lands as Tahiti or Turkmenistan, be loaded with greens or bankrupt, be endowed with the horse power of a 20-year-old youth or as depleted as a 70-year-old (Picasso is a rare exception, he was far from depleted), yet their reactions can be as similar as Siamese twins when it comes to responding to a pair of sexy legs – male, or female, depending on their inclinations.'

'Which way do you incline now, Antara?'

'I haven't changed, Adi. Not by that much. I have no qualms about experimenting, but my inclinations are firmly towards the male torso.'

'Have you experimented?'

She laughed. 'Have you, Adi?'

He, too, laughed, shaking his head.

Antara pulled the frail clip that had so far held the huge auburn mass on the top of her head. The cascading curls reached just till her breasts. *Are those yet that firm?* Aditya felt himself hardening. He suddenly realised the coffee shop had darkened. They were the only ones remaining in the place, other than the staff, who were busy preparing to shut for the night.

'It seems it's time for them to close,' Antara remarked.

Aditya looked at her. *What now, Antz?*

'How about dinner at my place, tomorrow?'

She can still anticipate my thoughts!

'It's just a dinner invite, Adi. Not to an orgy.' She laughed. 'Aah! I forget! Perhaps you need to check with your wife? London life kind of makes one forget these old subcontinental rules.'

Tina does not need to know of any of this. . . .

Aloud, he said, 'An orgy would have been far more fun, but I guess I will settle for a simple dinner. Where are you putting-up?'

'Once you have freshened up after work, just take the elevator down to the third floor in the other wing.'

'You are in the same complex! What exactly are you up to, Antara?'

'You will know. Come over tomorrow. If you don't turn up, I will not call to find out why. And I don't need a ride. I have a car waiting outside.'

Antara had just stepped out of the bath when the phone rang. It was Aditya.

'Antara, I will be there by ten. Had promised the kids a movie and McDonalds.'

'Sure. Ten is fine.'

'Bye then. See you'.

Show time, girlie!

Antara dried herself and applied another herbal face-pack to fill the intervening hour. Then she poured Ylang Ylang body cream generously over her satiny skin to make it softer . . . smoother . . . Her body, fragranced with the essence, smelt of desire. Next she un-wrapped the black satin Versace lingerie that she had bought after much consideration; its cost had been substantial; she was not one to spend money on frills unless some gain could be got out of it. She slipped it on and examined herself in the mirror. The deep curves, painfully maintained with strenuous gyming and tortuous diet regimes, had always seemed worth their while, but today Antara could not but pat herself mentally for the stunning results the mirror endorsed. Her dusky skin bore no trace of pigmentation and looked even more inviting against the black lace. She dabbed a little of the essence on her sensual curves, in her underarms, and on her inner thigh. She slipped into an ash-gray evening dress tailored from exquisite Italian silk. The cut, though simple, enhanced her curves. The deep neck narrowed down to a tight waist after which the fabric fell softly, clinging tautly to her shapely back. It ended just before her mid-thigh. Antara sat to notice its effect.

Just about hides the panty-line. Perfect!

She slipped on a pair of white pearl clip-ons, leaving her neck and hands bare. She tucked her well-cared for heels into a pair of high-heeled red sandals, open from the front allowing a peek of her well-shaped toenails, which were painted a deep maroon. She thickened her eyes with ash-kohl and wore a pale pink shade on her lips. She applied no rouge, nor any eye shadow.

Lastly, she examined her hair.

That single white hair must have been an aberration. I haven't glimpsed another in weeks.

Now she busied herself with the last-minute settings in her cosy living room. She lit the scented candles and burnt the lemongrass oil in the pot. She had chosen some CDs beforehand. Inserting one into the CD player (the VCR lay stashed in a cupboard) she adjusted the volume. Soft, seductive music filled the apartment, audible enough to create a mood but not loud enough to mar conversation. She placed the wine chiller, two small dishes of black and green olives, and two wine glasses, on the centre table. As she was slicing different varieties of cheese, the door-bell rang. Antara took her time in reaching the door.

Aditya was dressed in jeans and a casual t-shirt. In his hands he held a bunch of violet chrysanthemums.

'They are beautiful Adi, thank you', she murmured as she greeted him with a warm embrace. His hands touched her bare back and he smelt the powerful Ylang Ylang.

'Are you planning to kill me tonight?' he whispered in her ears.

'You called me a lioness last evening, didn't you?' she replied in the same bantering tone, making no move to break the closeness.

'Mmmm, the hunted is ready for the kill.'

'Lionesses do not eat dead meat, Adi. They spot their prey with great care and thrive on the game that ensues.' As she spoke, she led him inside by the hand.

Not this time, Antz darling!

'Your place smells as good as its mistress.'

'Thank you, monsieur. From both of us. Why don't you make yourself comfortable?'

'Since when have you been living here?' Aditya asked as he sunk into a deep and wide single seater sofa. There were no two seaters.

'I go to such lengths for you, Adi, and all that interests you is this steel and cement structure! Maybe Soft Solutions has taken more of a toll on you than I realised. Tell me, what can I serve you? Shall I pour you some wine?'

'Why wine, then? Have you forgotten what we enjoyed drinking when we meant serious business?' He threw the challenge back at her, enjoying the hunger she aroused in him.

'I have forgotten nothing. Give me a moment.'

As she went to fetch his drink, he couldn't take his eyes off her flawless rear. The dress was bare all the way to the tailbone. Her behind moved with cat-like grace.

Not an inch of extra fat! And as firm and well-contoured as ever!

Antara walked in with the bottle and poured him a large Laphroaig, neat. Back in the past, after her return from her first trip as an international air hostess she had got a bottle of it back with her. Till then Aditya had not even known that there was such a thing as a single malt scotch whiskey. He had loved its distinctive flavour. The sex afterwards had been torrid. After Antara left, Aditya had stopped drinking single malts.

She poured herself a small measure and moved towards Aditya. He made space for her and she squeezed in next to him on the single seater. Resting her back on the sofa she crossed her legs, allowing their thighs to rub. His gaze followed her legs and she saw a tug through his trousers.

They drank from their respective glasses. Aditya took in large gulps while Antara barely sipped, a tiny bit at a time. The music and the fragrance filled the room.

They conversed, as they had the previous day, with Antara doing most of the talking, her subjects as diverse and entertaining as before, still as unrevealing.

Aditya finished his drink and looked at her. She tilted her glass, finished hers, and extended the empty glass to him.

He rose and went to the table for their refill. Antara followed him with her eyes.

Aditya was wondering why Antara had made no reference to Tina, not asked him what excuse he had given her. He assumed she wouldn't know Tina was in rehab. But, of course, Antara knew. She even knew Tina would not be back for another three weeks.

Aditya soon finished his second drink. As he was about to get up, Antara shoved him down on the sofa with a gentle push. Taking the empty glass from his hands she kept it on a side table and murmured, 'Let me give you a shoulder massage first, Adi. I know how much you love one of those.'

Aditya slid back on the sofa and rested his head on it. She made her way to the back of the sofa and began at his nape. Before long, she tugged on his t-shirt. 'Take it off, my hands will work better on the nerves.' Aditya allowed her to pull it off but as he slid his hands on her breasts she gently moved behind the sofa purring 'What's the hurry? We have the whole night.'

Her deft perfumed hands worked gently down his back, and then made their way to the sides of his waist. With consummate artistry, her fingers commanded all his senses; he followed their movement, burning with feral desire. His front protested at this favouritism and he shifted his body to guide her hand where he wanted to be held. Taking the cue, Antara slid her hands to his upper chest and stroked his deep muscles, playing her way down to the waist. As she did so, her shoulders came to rest on his upper body. He smelt the perfume but also her skin. No sooner did her hands reach just below the waist and she would start all over again from the upper chest, pushing him to yet a higher level of urgency.

She is still so good at this!

As her hands reached his waist once again, he grasped her wrist and gave a sharp pull, drawing her towards him from the side. She crashed into his lap with feigned helplessness and hooked him in the eyes. Within moments, his mouth was on hers. He let his left-hand fingers slip to her buttocks and feel their fullness. With his right hand he fumbled in the silk, found her breasts, and cupped one.

Adiya soon finished his second drink. As he was about to get up, Antara shoved him down on the sofa with a gentle push. Taking the empty glass from his hands she kept it on a side table and murmured, 'Let me give you a shoulder massage first, Adi. I know how much you love one of those.'

Aditya slid back on the sofa and rested his head on it. She made her way to the back of the sofa and began at his nape. Before

Prashant let it rest at that and soon hung up, saying he would
drive down to visit them once Tina had settled down.
I wish I could tell you how right you are, Prats. What a horrid
Antara is in bed! And this time, it is she at the receiving end. . . .

29

Prashant had returned. He telephoned Aditya to enquire about
Tina .

On impulse – Aditya regretted it later – Aditya told him of
Antara's reappearance.

'Why did she pick your building amongst the zillion others?
It is not as simple as she makes it out to be. You have met her for
coffee once, fair enough! Now stay away from her, Aditya. Please!
You're playing with fire.'

'Prats! You are over-reacting. She is a non-issue now, okay? I
have a family I love and she knows that,' Aditya said, a little miffed
that Prashant still considered him to be the boy with a broken
heart.

'Did it stop her from breaking that man's marriage back then,
Aditya? Tina will be back in a week. She can't know that your ex-
wife is back – and that too in the same building!'

'Not the same building. She is in the other wing. And anyway,
there is *nothing* for Tina to know of! Relax, Prats. By the way, did I
tell you what the girls and I are planning for Tina's return?'

Prashant let it rest at that and soon hung up, saying he would drive down to visit them once Tina had settled down.

I wish I could tell you how right you are, Prats. What a hottie Antara is in bed! And this time, it is she at the receiving end. . . .

30

Tamanna and Shaswati made huge 'Welcome Back' and 'Missed You' posters for Tina's return. Aditya engaged professionals for an express cleaning job of their penthouse; the florist was asked to warm up the apartment with roses; he instructed Kantabai to prepare Madam's favourite *bhindi pyaz* and *tooer ni dal* for lunch. He had earlier bought two Burberry perfumes, taking delivery of one. This he placed on her dressing table with a brief handwritten note, 'Nice to have you back'. The other bottle was delivered to Antara's apartment with a bunch of orchids. There was no note, no indication as to the sender. It wasn't necessary.

'I should be back with Mom around two. Wear your prettiest clothes and sunniest smiles, girls!' Enthused by their father's cheerful disposition and happy that Mommy was coming home, the girls had worked themselves into a tizzy.

Tina returned home a bundle of nerves. Her face had aged as if by a decade in the eight weeks. She had lost kilos and her jeans hung around her limply. She looked unsure and lost. Though she responded to the fuss made of her, dutifully stretching her lips each time she felt it was expected of her, it was obvious that it was an effort rather than heartfelt.

But in the forty days that ensued, Tina experienced bliss as never before. Her decade of complaints against Aditya vaporised as he showered her with love, attention and care – much as he had done during their brief courtship and in the first months of marriage.

Aditya fussed over Tina, not as a patient requiring aftercare, but as a treasured girlfriend, whose every whim demands to be pandered to. Most evenings he returned home with small gifts: flowers, chocolates, wardrobe accessories and coordinates, books, theatre tickets, music albums. He planned outings: a husband-wife stroll on the seaside, a swim programme with the girls, dinner with friends whose company Tina enjoyed, a cosy family meal; once he even organised a picnic to Alibag. While at work he made regular calls to her, enquiring about her health, asking how her day was going. He wasn't just a listener, he told her how his day was going, shared gossip and news. He sent her texts; jokes, inspiring quotes, forwarded messages, engineered lines of love. One day Tina received a sophisticated camera, another day a courier delivered blank canvasses and extensive art supplies. Some days she got elegant cards reading 'I seek the pleasure of your company at China Garden at 8pm today' or simply 'Eros at 7 for *Angels and Demons*'.

In conversation he was cheery, bantering and attentive. Tina found her greatest pleasure in what he had not attempted in years: his teasing.

Tina was flummoxed, and quite delighted, when she received an SMS from him that read '*zipper is stuck, know anyone who may come in handy?*' She responded, '*I am good with chains.*' Of course, she did not know that he had forwarded the SMS he had received from Antara. And that he had forwarded Tina's reply in turn to Antara.

Not only did he respond enthusiastically to her overtures in bed he himself often initiated the love-making. There were nights when it was brief (*he's had a tiring day in office*) but there were also nights when the sex was prolonged and exhilarating, carrying Tina to heights of pleasure never before experienced.

During this period Antara once blindfolded him in bed. He tried it on Tina. Another occasion Tina urged him to break their record for the longest kiss. At their next assignation, Aditya challenged Antara to break theirs. He ordered a bottle of Dom Perignon for Antara and then arranged for Patchi chocolates to be delivered to Tina. He shopped for lingerie from Marks and Spencer's for Antara and picked up designer saris for Tina from the adjacent boutique.

'Aditya, I'd like to go to the opening of Pratap Varma's exhibiton at JJ Studio. I don't want to go alone. Will you come with me?' Tina asked Aditya over the phone one afternoon.

'Sure. What time is it?'

'Two hours from now. You'll have to leave office within an hour.' There was no immediate response from him and Tina prodded him in a hesitant voice.

'Aditya . . . If you're busy, I'll understand.'

'No. I have a meeting but it is not that important. It can be rescheduled. I will be there in an hour and a half.' Tina sensed the abruptness in his voice and cursed herself for the impulsive demand.

But perhaps his abruptness was not directed at me. Re-scheduling an important meeting at short notice can be quite bothersome. He is such a changed man! I think. . . .

She didn't allow the thought to run its course.

Aditya called Antara.

'Something has come up, Antz. I will have to take a rain-check today.'

'If you must, Adi. I had special plans for today. . .'

The seductive promise in her voice was quite clear to Aditya.

After a slight hesitation he said, 'I must, Antz.'

Disconnecting, Aditya felt the first burst of irritation with Tina since her return.

They were lounging in the living room of the penthouse after returning from the exhibition.

'Aditya, I know how much you love your sun-downers. You can make yourself a drink, really. I'll be okay. I *am* okay. There's no desire in me any more to touch alcohol. In fact, you can go to the pub with your friends if you want to. I'll be only too happy to do a family thing by myself with the kids.'

Aditya spent the evening in Antara's third-floor apartment in the other wing.

That night Tina wrote in her diary:

Today, he left his office and his work at my last-minute request and went to an exhibition with me. Leaving for the pub afterwards, he hugged me. I have finally earned his love! We are a happy family now.

The next afternoon, the bubble burst.

31

Tina answered the call on the landline in the penthouse.

'Is that Tina Malik?'

Tina didn't recognise the female voice. She answered, 'Yes, that's right. Who's this?'

'Never mind. Be at Taj, Colaba, at two in the afternoon tomorrow. The lobby in the new wing. Take care that you are not seen.'

'Excuse me!'

'Your husband will be there with Antara, his former wife.'

'What! Who's this? Where are you calling from? Hello! Hello!'

'Tomorrow, 2 p.m.'

The line went dead.

Tina shrugged her shoulders. 'People can go to any length to pull a joke. This is a bad one. Whoever's behind this, she needs a strong spanking.'

What if it is true?

It would explain Aditya's behaviour. . . .

Of course not! What Aditya is with me is the truth, my hard earned truth. The woman on the phone is a fraud, a mean prankster.

He was on the phone at 2 a.m. the other night. Business call to the U.S., he said. They have their day when we have our night.

His phone beeps with messages at all hours. That never happened before!

He's taken to looking at himself in the mirror in a certain way. . . .

The other day he made an appointment for a facial. He always used to wonder why men needed those. . . .

That day he returned from the office wearing sneakers. When Tamanna asked if he had been playing games in his office he was so startled! He looked at me so strangely. . . . telling me, not Tamanna, that he had started going to the gym. I thought he was doing it for me, but. . . .

All these years he stuck firmly to either beer or Black Label. Now he doesn't drink beer. Says it's fattening. These past forty days he's been having that strange new Laphroaig! He HAS changed!

Why would Aditya put up the pretence? Our marriage was not going great anyways. It would have been easier for him to tell me that he wants to get out of it. He didn't because his family, I . . . we mean something to him.

Our lovemaking has never been more passionate, I can feel his urgency. We kiss. . . .

Conflicts raged in Tina's mind.

The children, arriving home from school, sensed that their mother was disturbed about something. They discussed the matter in hushed whispers in the privacy of their bedroom, worried that she would have a relapse (Shaswati had to explain to Tamanna what it meant) and decided it was best they leave her alone.

In the evening Tina arranged for them to have a sleep-over at a friend's house.

Aditya returned home with the DVD of *Against All Odds*.

He looks as stupidly happy as he has done since my return. Can Antara be the cause?

They ate dinner alone. Aditya prattled away about his day and other little things. Tina's contribution to the conversation was mostly monosyllabic. Aditya thought her preoccupied and put it down to a mood swing.

Now they were lounging in the living room. The staff had left for the day. Aditya was readying to insert the DVD into the player.

'We need to talk, Adi.' Her voice was heavy, serious.

She marked the stiffening of his back as he stayed frozen for a moment, with the DVD in his hand.

'What's the matter?'

'Is Antara in Mumbai?'

'Aaaa . . . It is not the way you think. Uh . . . You see. . . '

His face had coloured. He was fumbling with the DVD. His eyes averted her. Tina cut him in mid-sentence.

'Is she here?'

'Yes. I was meaning to tell you Tina. Aaa. . .'

'You bastard! How long has this been going on?' Her voice bordered on hysteria. *I need a drink!*

'Tina, please! Calm down. It is not the way you think. Let us handle this as adults,' he implored, uncharacteristically defensive.

'What do you want to explain? What should I do now? Participate in a threesome, an orgy? Is that handling it like adults?'

'Tina!'

'Is she single?' Tina was almost screaming now. *I can't handle this without my vodka.*

'Yes. . .' Tina sensed a hint of indifference, the cold aloofness that she so feared, making its way into his tone.

'Oh! So after throwing you out years ago she has now decided that her ex-husband is not so bad after all, considering that he still waits on his knees, tongue hanging out, to welcome her back. Isn't it so? Isn't this your fucking reality? And you know what, I'm worse than you! I'm a bigger fool, for I wait for you with my tongue hanging out, too. Aah! I deserve you like you deserve her. A bloody fair God!'

Tina began laughing. There was no mirth in her laughter.

'Oh God! All that love making! It was because of her. Do you even visualise her when you fuck me?'

Aditya flung the DVD away. It flashed silver as it arced through the room.

Tina was now weeping.

'I'm leaving. We'll talk when you are in a better frame of mind.'

Aditya turned towards the main door of the penthouse.

Don't go, Aditya. Not like this. I'll kill myself. I swear to you, I'll kill myself.

But what she said aloud was: 'Go to her. At least then you won't have to close your eyes.'

'Perhaps that is exactly what I should do.'

Tina heard the door slam and collapsed on the sofa.

BOOK 3

32

Sprawling over three acres, an early 20th century construction, Aditya's Mahabaleshwar home had a typical colonial flavour. The driveway was long and winding, thick foliage in and around the grounds screened the bungalow from the hustle and bustle of the town. Here and there were small outhouses that had served as stables, tool-shed and staff quarters; that now had been turned into a garage and servants' quarters. The bungalow itself lay almost hidden under thick creepers and tall shrubs. A spacious verandah, with sloping tiled roofs, circled it on three sides. The back verandah had been built-over when a kitchen, storeroom and such, had been added by previous owners.

By lunchtime, all had arrived: Manas, Upasna, Poorvi and Kriya.

Each of them asked about Tina. Aditya told them Prashant Jha, his uncle and Tina's confidante, who would be joining them for lunch, would explain.

Manas was in the verandah when Prashant arrived. They were not strangers, having met on a few occasions at Tina's home.

'Prats! Where's Tina? She's not coming, is she?'

'No, Manas. She isn't. I'll explain after lunch.'

Lunch was an awkward meal. None had been in a conversing mood particularly after learning that Tina was not to be present.

After the meal they gathered in the verandah and made themselves comfortable in cane chairs arranged around a wooden table.

Prashant who was holding a parcel was the first to speak, 'Tina considers all of you to be her closest friends. She cares a great deal about all of you. And that is why she took this initiative. If she had mentioned in her letters to you that she would not be present herself you may not have come. Right now she is somewhere in these very hills . . . discovering herself.'

Each looked at the other and smiled, a smile which said that they all truly cared for Tina.

Prashant extracted a sealed envelope from the packet in his hands. On it was written in Tina's hand, '*For Aditya – To be read by Prats in Mahabaleshwar on the 10th of July in the presence of – Aditya, Manas, Upasna, Poorvi and Kriya.*'

'Tina's first letter is for Aditya. She has asked me to read it out. Without further ado, I shall begin.'

Aditya

In rehab, I had thought I was past my worst. The night I learnt of her return, after you walked out, I was sorely tempted to drown myself in vodka. The night was a black hole threatening to devour me. I was at an end. I could see no light or hope. I waited for your return, aware of each passing second, fighting my need for vodka.

The impulse to cut the hopeless wait with a stroke of the knife was overwhelming. Yet I convinced myself to hold on a little longer, sure that you would return. What I had seen in your eyes, before I went into rehab, was genuine.

I waited.

The night-silence is deafening. The compressor of the motor in the refrigerator swings into action every three minutes. The wooden skirting of the living room walls has eighteen nails holding them in place. The girl in the window opposite our living room, who walks as she reads late into the night, paces nine steps each side.

What if you had returned and told me you were sorry, that you only loved me, that Antara was a big mistake?

At sixteen minutes past four, the doorknob turned. You walked in. I saw it in your eyes, before you looked away guiltily. Anaesthetic numbs, vodka too, but that night your look numbed me. And then your words lacerated the numbness.

"Antara is back in Mumbai, Tina. She is okay with where she is. Our marriage does not need to go anywhere."

Ten years of loving you to madness. Ten years of praying, hoping – that some day you will love me back. And at last the final lap. I was never really in the race, only a filler.

You told me nothing had changed, that nothing needed to change, that I would continue to enjoy the monetary benefits, privileges, you. . . .

You said that you were not the first to have done so. You threw out names – but I didn't love any of those people, I loved you.

Where did I go wrong in my love for you, Aditya? What was my fault?

I still waited.

You came out of our bedroom with a pillow and blanket and walked towards the guest room.

'Look me in the eye, Aditya,' I wanted to scream.

But my lips refused to open. You didn't look at me. The click of the door behind you was like a shot into my chest.

The end of 'us', no more 'us', reverberated shrilly in my mind.

And then a delicious thought, banishing my pain. 'No me!'

For the first time that night, I felt calm, at peace.

I went up to our terrace, only conscious of the mantra 'No me!'

The night was not a malignant black hole; it was benignly beckoning me to immerse myself in its soothing shroud.

The air on the terrace was cool and fresh. I loved the way my hair responded to the sea breeze, dancing at its whim. I inhaled deeply; to live every second of what was left was important.

My mind kept playing, 'No me!' I went to the edge and looked down. The bright neon lights invited me to join them.

'A few more seconds please,' I pleaded.

Every little while, a lone car sped through.

The dogs chased after a sleek black car – a rich teenager returning home after a night-out with friends; or, a husband returning home to his wife after a night with his mistress.

A hatchback wove on the blacktop, climbed the kerb, and slammed into a tree. People gathered around; mostly security guards from the nearby buildings. They were shouting and gesticulating. A police jeep appeared followed by an ambulance and a Press van. White-clad figures extracted a body from the wreck. A stretcher disappeared into the ambulance. It raced away, sirens screaming.

Flashes of the injured tree and smashed automobile overwhelmed the neon lights. My colleagues, the photographers, were at work. Had they got the right angles, the best ones? Didn't they have any supplemental lighting? I hoped they had taken some mid-distance shots as well. . . .

Was he dead already? Will he live? It's too late for the day's papers; the news channels on television will have the answers by morning.

And then I remembered, I would not see the morning.

For a long time I stood there.

Suddenly, I realised the sky in the east had grown lighter. I climbed the parapet and looked down. Nothing stood between 'me' and 'No me!'

'What about the children? How will Shaswati and Tamanna live with it?'

'There is no better way to make Aditya pay for all that he has made you go through.'

'Step down, Tina; for their sake, if not yours.'

'Jump, Tina.'

Waves of conflicting thoughts crashed their way in. My mind was a churning sea hit by a squall.

Moments passed.

I could see the fine hair on my arms. Warmth enveloped me as the tempest raging within me abated. Looking up, I saw the golden light streaking through the eastern sky. A new day had been born.

I did not want to die. I wanted to live.

Returning to the penthouse, I found I had left the main door ajar. . . .

My mind had drawn its conclusions. Over the immediately ensuing days and nights it saved me time and again from sinking into the abyss my heart tried to drag me into. You see, my heart continued to belong to you, Aditya. It sought to explain away everything; it fought your case with persistence and ingenuity.

Those days I had stopped venturing out of the house, stopped accepting any telephone calls. I shunned my closest friends, .my parents, even Prats. I would sit with an empty sheet or canvas in front of me and be unable to find the energy or the inspiration to sketch or paint. I thought I would take still-life photographs of objects in the penthouse but an hour would pass fidgeting with the camera with the shutter remaining unclicked.

Lonely and depressed, unable to decide upon my next step, I sought escape in the chat rooms of the internet. Here I met Rohit.

In him I found a kindred soul, as lonely and depressed as I was. His business was going through a rough patch. The romance had gone out of his marriage even as his wife remained supportive. His children adored him and strove to comfort him through the troubled times. In spite of, perhaps because of, all the support he was getting from his family he was close to depression.

We connected. As virtual (pun intended) strangers, with no baggage of a shared past, we found it easy to confide in one another. I boosted his self-esteem. He in turn boosted mine. For one, the other was a stress-buster. We exchanged telephone numbers, discovered both of us lived in Mumbai. We began speaking to each other on a regular basis, making no attempt to meet in person.

Then Rohit sms'd one day, 'Away from you I'm bereft. Miss you a lot. What am I to do?' My heart skipped a beat. It has begun, I told myself. Or perhaps I'm reading too much into the words. I called him up. We chatted for a long time but neither of us referred to the sms.

A few days letter he again sms'd 'You consume my thoughts. I want to meet you.' Then he called, beginning with a couplet he had written for me. I was an angel that God had sent to keep him sane; he couldn't imagine life without me any more. I didn't know what to say. He went on with his astonishing declarations. He felt ashamed of himself. After all that his wife had done for him he felt that he was no longer fully hers; a part of him belonged just to me. 'I can't help my feelings for you, Tina. I love you,' he said.

I laughed into the phone, in pleasure.

I enjoyed his adoration of me; it made me feel pampered and cherished. I was grateful for his conversations, which physically filled up those empty hours when the kids were at school or otherwise occupied, when I felt most unwanted and alone.

Rohit became the medium through whom I revisited the days when I was indeed a princess; happy, pampered, and indulged by parents and family.

The future remained nebulous and undefined but in Rohit I found hope. He gave me back my optimism.

I was no longer miserable. You and I, Aditya, lived as strangers those long weeks; our interaction limited to the minimum necessary to keep the home running and children unaffected. Antara had slid into my side of the bed, which I had in effect vacated – with no attempt by you to lure me back. Perhaps that is why I did not regress into alcoholism! Strange, isn't it? When we know that there really is no one holding the fort for us, we own up to our defences.

The children were cheered with this more in-charge Mommy. In the home there was peace, if not contentment.

My ubiquitous obsession with unrequited love began receding as Rohit inched his way in with his couplets and sms's.

However emotionally stabilising Rohit was for me, I was well aware that he did not arouse in me feelings commensurate with the love he declared he had for me. Rohit was falling hopelessly in love with me, and I could see it.

One day he sms'd me: 'All that I want from you I already have. I am happy, Tina. Unless you desire more from our relationship. . .'

I did not reply. Since he did not ask for more, I did not give more.

Then things started changing. He became exacting, demanding.

'Did you think of me when you saw Cheeni Kum?'

'I was expecting you to call today.'

'Don't you feel like meeting me?'

In his messages was implicit an underlying query: 'When will you reciprocate my affections in the way I deserve?'

As his demands grew, so did my irritation. And at last I began to understand . . . Perhaps this is how it had seemed to Aditya!

Rohit and I were chatting on the phone. He asked me if I had missed his call the previous day. I had not; had in fact welcomed the break; but I couldn't tell him so. I turned the conversation to something else. A few minutes later he returned to his original query, saying even if I had not he wouldn't mind, but he'd like to know the truth. After a brief pause I told him 'Bye for now' and ended the call.

I was suddenly reminded of the time you, Aditya, had just returned after a week in Europe. I snuggled up to you, asked if you had missed me. You stayed silent for a while. Then you broke the embrace and switched the television to CNBC with 'what's happening to fuel prices?'

Another day I banteringly used the expression 'emotional adultery' for our telephone tête-à-têtes. Rohit went ballistic. He said I had insulted his love. Uttering 'Goodbye forever' he cut the connection. A few minutes later he sms'd 'I will never stop loving you. Best we stop all communication.'

I laughed to myself. I was sure he'd call within the week. He did, repentant, more effusive. The incident brought back the memory of another.

Aditya, I told you in a huff: 'I've had enough of your indifference. If you can't give me the love I deserve, I too withdraw my love for you. I'm going to my parents to think things out. I may not be back.' You smiled at my outburst, said nothing. An hour later I came to you, contrite and apologetic.

At last I understood. With Rohit, I was Aditya . . . the one not in love, the one without desire. For the first time I saw you, Aditya, as an individual in your own right; an individual separate from the way I wanted you to be. Your reactions and behaviour; your cry for space, your need for it; your irritation at my love-filled declarations – all became comprehensible. However much I doted on you, it was not in your hands to return the emotions in like manner.

I know now that these things are not in our hands.

I still spoke to Rohit, but more out of pity than anything else.

The boundaries between 'Tina the sufferer' and 'Tina the perpetrator' blurred; worse than the infliction unleashed by unrequited love is love doled out in charity. I came to dislike the Tina I was turning into.

My curse was not that I loved you, Aditya. It was what I had done to myself to get that love returned. Your not forgetting Antara I had taken to be my own lack.

You denigrated my legitimate need for love, for affection, and I took your side against mine. The more you shrugged, the clingier I got. Had I been able to completely break away from you – or from myself – I would have perhaps still lived in half-measures. But I could do neither. Whenever this internal strife became too much I sought refuge – in vodka, thoughts of suicide, a new relationship. . . .

At this point in my life I do not know the course I must take. However, I do know the course I must not. The destination remains unknown, but the direction is clear to me.

Someone has said: "To really love someone, you've got to get all worked up. When two are playing the game, it can be fun; but if you're playing it alone, it becomes silly."

I can finally see that it is not tragic, it is plain silly.

I wish you all the best, Aditya. I don't hold you responsible for our past.

Rohit? Last night I emailed him a poem I had written. As he understands the language of poetry I hoped reading it he would understand me. Today morning he called. We spoke for one last time. He had at last understood me. And that his happiness lies elsewhere. . . .

The poem:

Free at last!
Just when I thought I was doomed
To
Love
Desire
Crave
And wait
Knowing that it will never be returned
Just when I thought that life
Will always be a series of 'if only . . .'
Just when I thought that everything worthy

Be it a sunset, a performance or a song
Will never be beautiful for me
For he will be missing
Just when I thought that perhaps I should pray
For it all to be over
Breath
Feelings
Just when I thought I had lost
It poured
Peacocks danced
I smelt the Earth
And I did not think of him
His indifference
Finally did
What my years of persistence could not
I am free!

Aditya, my interaction with Rohit helped me to understand my own self. It helped Rohit in figuring himself out. And it helped me fathom you.

Aditya, in freeing Rohit I freed myself. And I hope I have freed you. . . .

33

Prashant asked to be excused for a moment. No one spoke. Aditya busied himself with lighting a cigarette.

Returning from the toilet Prashant heard laughter. Happy laughter. Emerging on the verandah he hard Aditya speak three words that cheered him immensely ' . . . *happy for Tina.*'

Resuming his seat, he nodded at Aditya. They exchanged smiles.

That's my boy! Bless you, Tina.

Clearing his voice, he read out the next letter:

Manas, Poorvi, Kriya, Upasna: As in my times of deepest despair, so when I made peace with myself, I thought of all of you.

You are wondering why 'this'? I could have explained individually to each of you.

My friends, 'this' is not about myself solely, or about Aditya and me alone. That would have served only my purpose, or Aditya's and mine.

My friends, 'this' is about the 'us' that we are. We are all part of one huge whole. We complement each other.

None of us is alone in feeling what we do. Facts may differ, but we all have our troubles.

Speaking of our dilemmas and our burdens to another, in trying to make another understand, we understand our own selves. And as we try to understand the other's dilemmas and the other's burdens, we begin to understand our own selves.

One, then, needs the other.

One can only be free when the other is free.

It is with this self-realisation that I have taken the liberty of asking you to be here.

None of you are strangers to each other. Each here is the 'other' too. Speak, my friends. Tell it from the beginning. And listen.

Prashant handed Upasna a sealed envelope.

34

Dear Upi,

*As much as we women are pampered within the secure walls
of our rich and cultured homes, we are also made to internalise
the necessity of compromise, tolerance and forgiveness as the
custodians of lasting marriages. The message, though tacit, is
categorical: 'lasting' is exclusively the wife's responsibility. Cut
across religions, economic strata, groups, bias of caste or creed,
of the one billion plus force that we are, most unite unanimously
on this one issue. We women perpetuate this fallacy and lug the
burden even when it leads us to the funeral pyre.*

*I ask of you today: How much will you take? When will it be
enough? Where will it end for you? Is it worth it?*

*Love
Your Tinee*

Reading the letter, Upasna had not removed her oversized
sunglasses. Now she took them off. With the tip of a finger she

trailed the deep gash running from the tail end of her right eyebrow to where the cheek bones began.

It happened gradually, Tinee. So much so that it was only natural to accept what came my way.

Upasna looked at the others and spoke.

'Once our elders had approved of the match based on the usual parameters, and our *janamakshars* – horoscopes – had been tallied, our families met. I had previously seen Umesh's photograph but seeing him in person I was dazzled. He looked dashing in his suit. These *dekha-dekhi*s are very public affairs with families out in full force, cousins and all. We barely managed to exchange a few words. It was anyway difficult with eavesdropping kin all around you. Umesh petitioned our elders to be allowed to speak privately to me. It was a bold request considering the circumstances. Umesh had scored a perfect '10' with the elders of my family. They agreed with alacrity and we went for a drive.

'I asked him if he hadn't met interesting NRI girls while studying at Stanford in the U.S. NRI girls are half-baked Indians, neither here nor there, he said. He had always been clear only a truly Indian girl who had grown-up with authentic Indian values could be his wife. By the time our allotted hour ended I had him pegged as a little arrogant, quite self-assured, very well-mannered and definitely decent man. Returning home I gave my assent.

'We waited for the reply from Umesh's family. When it did not come immediately our elders became perturbed. They worried that somehow Umesh's family had learnt of my sister Suniti's problems – her marriage was on the verge of breaking-up and she had been instructed to pull along till my engagement. Those days, particularly in our community, a sibling's broken marriage had great stigma attached to it. My parents were tense. I too became anxious. Finally we were informed that it was a go-ahead.

'The engagement ceremony was a grand affair. Umesh was the envy of all my friends. Numerous relatives complimented me on my catch. Those with marriage-age daughters of their own were envious of my parents. Slipping a 7-carat heart-shaped diamond ring onto my finger he whispered "You are breathtakingly beautiful." I was thrilled. I truly felt lucky and sent up a silent prayer of thanks to the almighty.

'Our engagement period was brief, just about a month. My days were filled with shopping and visits to and from jewellers, dressers, etc; evenings with parties and dinners. Umesh flew down on the weekends. One evening we were parked in a remote corner of a basement car-park in a mall. He pulled my face to his and kissed me. It was my first time. Eyes shut in ecstasy; I led his palm inside my kurta – as I had seen in the Hollywood movies. As the tips of his fingers came in contact with my skin he pulled away with a jerk, almost tearing my kurta. Opening my eyes I saw disgust plainly written on his face. He started the car and said "We are defined by our roots, Upasna. Our roots do not allow us this freedom. Your parents have placed their trust in me. I am not so blinded by lust that I will take advantage of their faith in me." His tone was scathing, his words, acid. I was chilled to the bones, and felt like a slut.

'I wanted to defend myself, tell him that I too believed in chastity before marriage, that I loved him; that as we were getting married soon, I didn't think it was wrong to just feel each other. But all I said was "Sorry" in a meek, contrite voice. Dropping me off he admitted, his voice much softer – he too had wanted it as much as I, but traditions had to be respected beyond impulses and desires. That night I tossed and turned in bed. For the first time doubts assailed me. Had I done the right thing in saying yes to him? But eventually I convinced myself that he had been right. I cheered up at the thoughts of his nobility. I told myself, 'Perhaps he is conservative, but he is perfect husband material. He will never fool around the way some men do.' I slept.

We got married.'

Upasna fell quiet. She was thinking of that first night. . . .

The passion with which they made love . . . his concern about not hurting her . . . falling asleep in his arms . . . the thump in the night . . . waking up . . . seeing Umesh sprawled on the floor . . . Umesh getting up . . . his anger . . . his harsh words.

The slap, whose sting she felt even after all these years. . . .

Umesh had returned from the bathroom, got into bed without a word, and gone to sleep. Lying sleepless in bed she had recalled the little warnings of the past month which she had failed to heed.

Prashant coughed discreetly. Upasna sighed, returning to the present.

'Subtly but gradually I had changed, even during our short engagement, giving in a little more each time to his all-consuming, annihilating, orthodox and chauvinistic male ego. He would say:

"Is it necessary to wear such a low cut dress, Upasna? Do you want to flaunt your assets and attract male attention?"

"Don't giggle so. Maintain your grace. You are soon to be a Mishra Bahu."

"My brother-in-law will be coquettish with you. It is up to you to be smart enough to handle him."

'But I still perceived only the many positives in him. The reality of what I had got into hit me on our very first night. After we had made love we fell asleep. In the middle of the night he got up to go to the bathroom, stumbled over my slippers and fell. The sound woke me up and I switched on the bedside lamp. He got up and screamed at me, accusing me of carelessness. He slapped me.

'In the morning he didn't speak of the incident but his actions conveyed more than an apology, or so I thought. He was charming, indulgent, and gave me the I-have-eyes-only-for-you kind of look. My hurt melted under his loving gaze.

'Perhaps it had been my fault. I should have put my slippers by my own bedside rather than at the foot of the bed. And so, easily, I excused him and implicated myself.

'As I justified his mistreating me, he gave me more of it in liberal doses, often worse than the previous ones.

'We were on our honeymoon in Austria. Umesh was driving. Neither of us was any good at deciphering maps. We got lost. I suggested asking someone for directions. He just continued driving. As I once again broached the idea of seeking guidance he braked suddenly and instinctively I reached out to brace myself on the dashboard. I sprained my wrist. The sixth evening of our honeymoon we spent at the doctor's. He bandaged my wrist and gave me pain-killers. There was nothing wrong with my legs but he insisted on carrying me in his arms back to the hotel. Once in our room he insisted I lie down while he fussed around. We ate dinner in the room and he practically spoon-fed me even though I protested I was perfectly capable of feeding myself. As I lay in bed he fetched a glass of water for my pain-killers and started off. "I love you, Upasna. More than you can imagine. But your doubting my abilities to find my way irritated me. A wife should have faith in her husband"

'At that moment I felt contrite. I apologized. He *had* eventually found the way to our destination. I should have been more patient.

'Some weeks after our return home, I invited a childhood friend over for dinner who was in Delhi on a short visit. She had a companion with her so I invited him too. After conversing desultorily for a while Umesh became uncharacteristically quiet.

Midway through dinner he walked off. Once my guests had gone I hurried to our bedroom and asked him what was wrong. "What's wrong with *you* to invite such people over? That cheap fellow couldn't keep his hands off her. I bet those hippies aren't even engaged!" I became angry myself. I told him they were on the verge of getting engaged but it was anyway their private matter. No concern of ours. He had insulted my friend by walking out as he had, with no explanation. What had happened to his much flaunted belief in traditional values. *Atithi Devo Bhava.*

'This was the first time I had answered back to him. He twisted both my hands behind my back with one hand. With the other he grabbed the back of my head and banged my forehead against the wall. I fainted. When I revived I found myself in his arms. He was applying a cold compress to the lump on my forehead. I pressed the spot and the pain was bad. I shed silent tears. He said he was sorry. He hadn't meant to hurt me. But the fact remained we had a family name to keep, we could not associate with people who indulged in live-in relationships. The two of us were not separate but one. Each was responsible for upholding the principles of the whole.

'Of course, what he was really saying was that as the man his principles were predominant. As the woman, the wife, it was my duty to uphold his principles even if I didn't agree with them.

'That night he was especially sweet to me. A few days later he again lost his temper over something and again hit me. And again he was immediately contrite and consoling. That night, as I lay in his arms, I rashly broached something that had been troubling me. I said "Umesh, I know Papaji hits Mummyji too. Perhaps that's why you do it too. It could be a psychological thing. Perhaps we should see a doctor, seek help." I felt his body stiffen. The hand lying on my stomach, which had been gently caressing me, clenched into a fist. He grabbed my jaw and bore his eyes into mine. He saw the fear in my eyes and I the primal gleam of triumph in his. At that moment I finally realised the horrible truth. What I had seen as aberrations, rationalised as momentary lapses, was my own foolish self-deception. *This* was the real Umesh. The other loving Umesh was the aberration. There was no reasoning with *this* Umesh. His words then shot through me like fire. "Your sister came back, right? You are free to leave too. Perhaps your family is used to their girls returning."

'I contrived a trip to my parents in Calcutta. I was sitting with Ma. Without going into the dreadful details I tried my best to explain how bad things were. No crying, but my eyes begged her to acknowledge the bruise on my forehead. She enquired about the usual things. Was he into drugs? Other girls? I told her a little more. She didn't seem to get it. Finally, in exasperation, I told her he was a wife-beater as was his father. I pointed to the bruise on my head and told her it was his doing. I told her I feared him, that perhaps the marriage was a mistake.

'Ma's face lost all colour. I saw dread and helplessness in her eyes as she said, "You too want to come back, like Suniti? Two girls and both back . . . What have we done to deserve this?"

'I did what I was trained to do. Place her concerns over mine. As she had placed ours before hers, all through my years in that house. So I backtracked. My words sounded strange to my own ears as I defended Umesh, more emphatically than I had implicated him. "No, Ma. That is not what I meant at all. We had this fight the other day and I guess I overreacted. Umesh is very good to me most of the times. He has eyes only for me, Ma. He never looks at another woman. Did I tell you how he insisted I buy the Rolex when I was only too happy with the dancing Chopard? He also told Mummyji that I can wear tracks to the gym. He is making space for me, Ma. He is good, really. If I don't contradict him, if I am what he wants me to be, he'll be the most considerate and loving husband. I guess it's up to me to make things work."

'Ma seemed relieved with my take. Her eyes lit up. "Plan a child. That'll soften him. It'll make him more pliable, you'll see."

'From Ma's room I went to Suniti's. She heard me out and told me point blank that I would be a fool to divorce a man such as Umesh just because I couldn't put up with a little violence now and again.'

Again Upasna fell silent. She was reminiscing. . . .

Suniti, do you remember that speech I gave the final year in college on Domestic Violence in India?

"In 2002 UNICEF published a report. Some of the statistics:

India has the highest rate of violence during pregnancy.

45 percent of Indian women are slapped, kicked or beaten by their husbands.

74.8 percent of the women who report domestic violence attempt suicide.

Every 6 hours a young married woman is burnt, beaten to death or driven to suicide.

Their survey lists the following as reasons for domestic violence:
Wife neglects the children
Wife goes out without telling her husband
Wife argues with her husband
Wife refuses sex with husband
Wife burns the food.

A survey by the International Institute for Population Studies showed 56% of Indian women believed wife beating to be justified in certain circumstances, that a woman's risk of being slapped, kicked or beaten rose with her level of education.

When will this atrocity stop? Who will stop it? We are the women of a new century. We are modern, educated, and confident. We are the privileged ones. It is our duty to help our weaker sisters.

We must remind our sisters: No one can treat you like a doormat without your consent.

We must tell our sisters: Stand up for yourselves!"

For the benefit of her listeners she summarised the speech and continued.

'Suniti laughed at the end of my speech. It was humourless, bitter. "Grow-up, dear sister. We were young and naïve. Life is not so simple. Do you really understand the alternative? I am a divorcee. I know."

'The circles we moved around in, that we thought refined, cultured, educated and liberal, had treated Suniti shabbily. The very qualities – youth, beauty, and the *bindaas* attitude – that had been her assets before marriage had now become her liabilities. Wives, even those who had been her friends before, perceived her as a threat, as someone who could lead their husbands astray. Perhaps they were correct. These husbands would message her on afternoons, on workdays asking her out for coffee. Some even had the audacity to add perhaps she needed a man "to discuss issues with." No one defended her as her reputation was torn to shreds – why take useless *panga* over a divorcee? And all of this behind her back: they still continued to invite her on weekends. Even relatives and well-wishers were not above maligning her. Suniti's divorcee status automatically carried the tag 'available for a short ride.' She had always been an extrovert. Earlier that had been perceived as her social asset. Now it was a 'put-on', 'to attract the opposite sex'. There were some who sympathised with her – but not with any empathy, only with pity. They looked upon her as a

166 | *All and Nothing*

lost cause, doomed to live a lonely life with little chance of real
happiness. The failed marriage had devalued all her credentials.

'On parting Suniti told me: "It is not about him Upi, it is about
you. If you can say 'fuck you' to this hypocritical society, if you can
be your own person without a man in your life there is no reason
why you should put up with this nonsense. If you can't, then you
are better off getting abused by one man rather than opening a
hundred other doors. . ."

'I flew back to Delhi the next day, back to my in-laws house,
resigned to my fate.

'I became pregnant. As Ma had predicted things did change
for the better. For a year and more the beatings stopped, except
for the occasional slap. Shanay was born. In him I found my salve.
He healed my soul, filled up the chasms. Umesh was the perfect
father. He did not resort to violence with his son. Nor did he
ever lift a finger upon me in Shanay's presence. If Shanay wasn't
around and he happened to lose his temper I fared the worse for
it. Shanay's birth had given me inner equanimity. I devised new
and ingenious ways to manage the outside. I became more adept
at reading his moods and ensuring Shanay's presence at those
times when he was at his worst. I took to wearing dark shades.
They hid the occasional black eye. Even in peak summer I took
to wearing full sleeves. They hid the occasional bruises on my
arms. I had never been a great one for make-up. I became a heavy
user. Those times when none of these sufficed I complained of
a migraine attack. It meant I could stay in my room for hours
together. I became an expert liar.

"How clumsy of me; descending, I missed a stair."

"I held it so tight that the thin glass gave way and broke in my
hand."

"I bumped my head on the cabinet."

Upasna unwrapped the dupatta. Her throat and neck revealed deep finger marks.

"Oh . . . you won't believe what happened the other night! Thieves broke into our house. They would have choked me to death had Umesh not given them the keys."

Upasna laughed mirthlessly. 'I'm so good at cooking up stories that I too believe them. Umesh's reputation stays intact. Shanay's belief in the good and beautiful stays unbroken. My parents can keep up their pretences. Life goes on smoothly.'

'Smoothly for everyone but you, Upasna,' Kriya intoned.

~

In the hills. . . .

Tina was in the forest amidst pallid leaves which hung limply on scarred black-brown boughs. The air was clammy and heavy, the sky a mass of grey shades.

Everything was still. She could see none of the forest creatures, nor could she hear any. The only thing with any movement seemed to be just herself. And she kept stumbling on the uneven ground scattered with stones, fallen branches and wayward roots. Her body brushed against jagged edges and thorns to cover it with cuts and scratches

Tina was miserable.

But she kept going . . . kept looking for a scurrying squirrel . . . the flowers lost in the overwhelming gloom . . . kept straining to hear the rustle of leaves, the call of the birds. Her stride did not flag and she willed herself to breathe evenly. It just got more oppressive, darker, heavier.

She had come here to be alone with her Maker. She had finally let go of him who was not hers. She now needed to know who she was without him. Did she still have within her beauty and wholeness? Did she have any self-worth left? Did she still have hope – *Can I go on? More importantly, should I go on?*

35

Dear Kriya

Pandit Jasraj once said in an interview: you can cheat the world, you can even cheat God, but you can't cheat yourself.
And you have been unable to. You keep flipping through the pages of the album of the past. Kriya, what your album needs are fresh pages. You need to create new photographs.

Love,
Tina

As she finished reading, Kriya burst out laughing. The others waited in puzzled silence. Kriya refolded the sheet and returned it to its envelope, which she put in her purse. Then she began.

'Tina and I were very good friends indeed! But I had no idea she had intuited so much. We shared a lot but our confidences never ran this deep. I have never spoken aloud to anyone, ever, of the turmoil that rages within me. Never.'

She adjusted the kalamkari dupatta over her shoulders.

'I was barely ten years old when my father was felicitated at a gala event in Bombay for being the first Indian fashion designer to exhibit in Paris with grand success. I had accompanied him from Pune, where we lived. "Princess," he said, "come here." I went and stood by him. Taking hold of my hand he spoke to the assembly of the best and the brightest of the Indian fashion industry. "Kriya, my princess, will be a greater designer than me. Not just Paris, Milan and New York will honour her. She has more talent than me." The people clapped as we hugged.

'My father doted on me. He really believed it, that I had immense promise. I thought so too. I attended this liberal arts school in Pune where the entire curriculum was designed to promote creativity; academics took second place. There were no examinations, not till the higher classes. We were randomly evaluated by our teachers, based on class work. That comprised drawing, painting, and simple craft work such that children can handle. We went for nature walks and visited museums and craft melas. We were encouraged to explore and experiment with colours, forms, materials and thoughts; to dream and give full vent to our imaginations. At home I had private tutors and my father kept me supplied with whatever tools and supplies were required, including art magazines and journals. There were regular soirees at our house or his studio where the doyens of the fashion world attended Papa's court and danced attendance to him.

'At school the teachers competed with each other in their praise of me and my class work. The rare ones who didn't were either prevailed upon by the school authorities to rectify their remarks or were just assumed to be mavericks. Papa was the Chairman of the Board of Trustees administering the school. At home the private tutors similarly were lavish in their praise of me. They needed Papa's patronage. Guests at the soirees or visitors to our house or papa's studio, who may or may not have seen any of the trifling stuff I was doing at the time, routinely spoke admirably of my talent to Papa – some out of plain courtesy, some to curry favours, and some perhaps really believed what they said.

'As I grew up Papa took to involving me deeply into his activities, particularly on holidays from school. I would accompany him everywhere – cutters, weavers, embroiderers, printers, etc. He would make me sit in with him when working on designs and materials or when clients came by. He would not only explain all the nitty-gritty of fashion designing, he would also solicit my opinions. I've always had good powers of observation and recall. All that I would do is to try and think back to a similar situation. Mrs Sinha is tall, slim and fair; so was Kangana Devi for whom Papa had chosen such and such. Papa would be impressed at my selections. Colour of a dress for a dance sequence in a film for an up-coming starlet? Maroon – I had overheard him say the week before maroon became the new colour of the season.

'By the time I was 15, I was adept at reading Papa's mind and I would give him the answers I thought would please him the most. He never realised it, that I wasn't expressing my own opinion, that I didn't *have* an opinion of my own. His own ego, his love for me, blinded him to what was happening. And I? I cared only about making him happy, making him proud of me. If he's happy with me, if the most illustrious fashion designer of the country is proud of me, I must of course be a great budding designer! Everyone says I'm very promising!

'With my good memory I did well in academics. Our Indian system of education rewards learning by rote, and that came easily to me. So I sailed through school. An inkling of my reality came to me only when I failed the admission test for NEXT, the famous fashion design institute in Pune. Papa was very angry. Not with me, with the institute. He called up the head of NEXT, a man who owed favours to my father. The next day I filled up the admission form.

'Then began the battle with my own mediocrity.

'Technique and theoretical concepts presented no problems for me. They had been drilled into me almost from birth. Copying and duplicating I could do masterfully. I had had enough training in that. But any assignment that entailed beginning from scratch, where one's originality was at test, found me floundering. Like other students who were similarly challenged I put it down to a lack of inspiration, an off day, or just simply blamed the instructors – they were not ingenious enough to understand my creation, or they were biased against me, they indulged in favouritism. Repeated remarks of 're-work', 'unclear' and 'unsatisfactory' accumulated. I began to notice other students who had initially been as much at sea as I had, progressing; occasionally even receiving the approbation of the instructors. I was smart enough to see the outstanding originality of some of the more talented students. The more simple ones I would occasionally charm or entice into helping me, even doing some of my assignments. Then the first year results were announced.

'That was the worst evening of my life. I saw my father crumble in the face of my evaluation reports. His princess had failed him. He didn't say a word to me, and averted to look me in the eye. That night he stayed awake till very late, something very unusual for him. Creeping past his study I saw him scribbling in his diary. He did that only when he was disturbed. Lying sleepless in bed I heard voices from the drawing room. He was watching television, which he considered a mindless pastime. I knew the big question eating him up was *where had he gone wrong?*

'I spent the next few days in his studio and prepared my portfolio for re-evaluation. He had assigned a team of designers to *assist* me. So it was that my father became my accomplice in the lie that would be perpetrated. I, of course, was thrilled. I thought my battle with mediocrity was over. Papa would *always* take care of everything. And if not he, I would find someone else.

'As expected, the re-evaluation went without a hitch. The day I was to begin the second year classes my father told me casually over breakfast that his team would henceforth be assisting me with my work. Of course, it should be kept under wraps, a secret.

'There was a girl in my class, Smita, a simpleton from some small town in Maharashtra. She was one of those who had a natural talent for originality. I had befriended her in the first year and she was one of the girls I got to help me from time to time. She had zero personality, terrible English, and was quite in awe of me.

'With Papa's team working behind the scenes on my projects and assignments, and Smita or one of the other kids helping me when the team couldn't, I sailed through the second year. From C+ my evaluations climbed to A+. In short, my performance zoomed. I now became a top ranker. The end of the second year I ended up a star student of NEXT.'

Kriya laughed, sipped some water from a glass, and after a brief pause continued.

'On graduation day I was awarded the gold medal. Accepting the award I announced the launch of Kriya Creations.

'At our celebration party that night I invited six of my batch mates to join KC. Over the past few months I had carefully selected them for their specific talents. So what if I lacked originality! So what if I lacked creativity! I could pick a good work from a hundred sketches with unerring accuracy. I had an instinct for recognising talent in others that exceeded even my father's. I had used these abilities to the hilt during my years in NEXT. I now planned to use them to build a name for myself. Since that terrible evening my father had not once called me his princess. I would make KC succeed so well that he would once again be proud of me. I would again be his princess.

'To get back to my story, Smita of course accepted my offer immediately. To the others I had made offers specifically modelled to their particular situations. All accepted. Smita, however, was the key to my future. Not just because of her natural talent, not just because I could manipulate her easily. Over the years as co-students I had dropped all pretence with her. She knew me as I was and accepted me as I was. In her I had found a true friend. My only friend.

'KC Unveiled, the name I gave to my debut collection, was a resounding success.

'I had read Smita correctly. The ensembles receiving the most accolades were all hers. At the celebration party, even as I stood accepting the plaudits of the fashion pundits, she remained with the others in the background, with a foolish smile on her lips. Throughout the evening I kept a watch on her. With her plain looks she attracted little attention. If anyone tried to speak to her she became nervous and fidgety. Speaking to someone she inevitably started stammering. Bored with her monosyllabic answers the person soon moved away.

'Our relationship deepened thereafter. She was not only incredibly creative, she was a genuinely nice person – soft in her gestures, simple in her affections, incapable of manipulation, as innocent as only someone from a small town can be. It was easy to love Smita, and for that reason I hated her. She was everything I would have liked to be.

'We both knew I was the boss but I didn't just want to be one because of my position, I wanted her to acknowledge that I was indeed superior to her in everything, other than in creating raw designs. I wanted to own Smita, own not only her designs, but the person behind those designs. She had to be my admirer, my cupboard – where I could stuff skeletons -- and a friend who would see the wrong in me and still love me.

'Thus began my mind games with her. One day I took her with me to visit a slum where I had donated some money for the repair of roofs. The grateful residents practically kissed the floor I walked on. Smita, as expected, was duly impressed. In the car on the way back she told me how surprised she was – and how happy to be working with me.

'Smita's father had a medical condition. On my insistence Smita called her parents to Pune. I arranged for their stay and personally accompanied them to our family *vaid* and started him on Ayurvedic treatment. The three months or so they stayed in Pune I monitored and paid for everything. On his departure he held my hand and told me I was a great soul, how lucky his daughter was to be working for me, etc.

'I made her join a Spoken English class and took her with me to my hairdressers. I bought her an entire new wardrobe with accessories and taught her to dress better. In short, I whipped her personality into better shape. Whenever and wherever I travelled for work she accompanied me.

'Of course I worked her hard and took full credit for her creations. I thought it a fair exchange. I gave her what she lacked and she made up for my shortcoming. She seemed quite happy with the arrangement.

'Even as I hated Smita I loved her, and needed her. She was the only one whom I thought I could trust to be my confidante. I had married young, soon after launching KC. A man my father chose for me. The only good thing that came of that mistake was my son, Yash, born within a year of the wedding. Soon after his

birth I filed for divorce. My father was very angry with me. All that
I had left was Smita.

'But she gave me more reasons to hate her than love her.
She was a mirror in which I saw myself turn uglier by the day.
I used every opportunity to shred her innocence, corrupt her
faith in goodness, make her a willing model to this new paradigm
where success pre-supposes deceit and hypocrisy, where she would
be driven to make those very choices. But however much she
compromised, there was something noble about her that I could
neither touch nor destroy.

'Soon after my divorce I moved to Mumbai and set up Elan. I
transferred Smita to Mumbai, arranged a place for her to stay.

'Time flew by. We were in Monte Carlo for a fashion event. I
liked an ensemble done in layers by an Italian. I thought it could
be adapted to Indian requirements and could be quite the thing for
the upcoming winter season. Smita told me of an Indian colleague
attending the event mentioning that his fashion house, Shivangi,
was considering the layered look for their winter collection. The
layered look was mine, I would not allow it. That evening I met
the editor of a leading Indian fashion magazine over dinner. She
wanted a chunk of our advertising budget. I honey-talked her
into agreeing to de-track Shivangi's plans. The next day I asked
Smita deliver to this editor an ensemble she had drooled over.
Advertisements I would give her.

'We were the only ones with a layered look for that winter.
The fashion editors and reviewers praised my foresight. KC was the
toast of the fashion world.

'Smita approached me one day. The girl had apparently
smartened up. She had put two-and-two together and wanted to
know if I had used her information to sabotage Shivangi's plans. I
told her of course I had. To succeed in the fashion business it is not

enough to just innovate, one has to be ahead; and if need be, as it was in this instance, competition must be eliminated. Given half a chance they would have done the same thing to me! The stupid girl protested weakly, asking if it was 'ethical'. But she didn't really have much to say.

'I decided it was time to put Smita through a litmus test. That very evening I introduced her as my leading designer to a leading film producer-director, a known debauch, and mentioned I was considering launching a Smita Sharma label under the KC aegis. Perhaps we could introduce her with one of his upcoming films. I looked at Smita and asked her what she thought of the idea. For moments I watched as conflicting emotions racked her. Concerns of virtue or rules of pragmatism – which would win out? The latter won. This bird had grown wings and wanted to fly. I hid well the triumphant feeling that coursed through me. Smita had learnt well from her tutor, me. She assumed a grateful smile and thanked me for the opportunity I was promising her and told the *filmwallah* she would be delighted to work with him.

'Thereafter I played her like a stringed instrument. I kept talking about launching her label without really doing anything about it. Whenever anyone was to be manipulated or bribed I used Smita. I forced her to lie to suppliers, co-workers, and clients. I made sure she experienced the worst side of the fashion industry. I no longer veiled from her my own darkest side. For weeks I watched the pain of self-conflict racking her. Even as her work deteriorated I promoted her with a substantial raise. By then it didn't matter to me. KC was well established, the money was rolling in and I had fresh talent working for me. Smita had outlived her usefulness as a creator, but I needed her for myself.'

Kriya fell quiet, playing with a pearl earring. She flicked an imagined fleck of dust from her sleeve and began speaking again, her voice flat.

'Then one day she came to me. The *filmwallah* had called her. He wanted to meet her to discuss the costumes for his forthcoming film, at his flat late in the evening. I told her I had spoken to the man. That very morning I had told him I had decided to launch the Smita Sharma label. I told her she should go. He was one of the most successful filmmakers in the country and his latest blockbuster was soon to go under production. It was an opportunity not to be missed. Reluctant at first, she soon got persuaded.'

Again Kriya was silent. She sat very still. Moments passed.

'Where is she now?' Manas asked.

'Dead. That night she hung herself from the ceiling fan in her room. Her suicide note said that no one but she was responsible for her actions, that she was just too depressed with life.'

Poorvi was unable to restrain herself. 'Did she go to that man?'

Kriya shook her head. She fidgeted with her hands in her lap.

'She hung herself with a sari. I can't work on the six yards any more. Dupattas, too. They knot themselves in strange ways before my eyes and refuse to loosen up. I see purple-blue marks on the fabrics I work upon. They choke me. All old men I see have her father's face. He had to come to collect the body. I can't forget his face . . . I can't meet my own eyes looking in a mirror. I turn a little uglier every day.'

Kriya touched her face, looked at the others and, voice-breaking, asked, 'Do you all see it too?'

No one looked at her.

Manas was the first to break the tension. He beamed at Kriya as he spoke.

'I see a beautiful woman trapped in an old photograph. Tina is right. You need to create a new one.'

In the hills. . . .

The silent forest seemed to leer out at Tina, providing her with no answers.

Maybe I should just surrender myself, give-up, allow nature to be my grave. Wasn't I soul-dead anyway?

She inhaled deeply. A coughing fit racked her.

'Let me just suffocate to death!' she screamed out into the murk. Unfeeling, uncaring nature responded to her rant with the silence of the dark forest. She was alone, horribly alone, and would be so for the rest of her life.

Was it always like this?

NO! I was full of life, people like me, love me, enjoy my company. I have deeply caring friends. It is I who have distanced myself from their warmth. How did I allow this to happen? Like this forest, does life too become stifling not in one huge sweep but in bits and pieces? Till every last desire and hope dies? Is all that one can do is, wait for the end stoically?

36

Manas, I want you to answer just two questions.

Do you believe Dwit loves you less because she chose to explore the alternative her family proposed – and perhaps reason dictated – or do you believe she loves you more after having given this alternative a fair chance; thus realising nothing was more important to her, neither certainty, nor finances, nor societal propriety, than you are?

Has not your ego claimed a high price in both your sufferings? How long will you allow it to rule you? How long, Manas?

Manas looked up after a long pause. His gaze went beyond the others, as if someone was in the garden beyond. He began humming, '*tomra je bolo dibasho rojoni bhalobasha bhalobasha . . . sokhi bhalobasha kare koi, seki keboli jatonamoy*'.

Then he began speaking.

'Dwit often urged me to sing this song for her. She grew up with Carnatic music, I with Rabindra Sangeet. . . .

'Dusky Wild Intelligent Temperamental – D-W-I-T, my Gayatri . . . I am from the east and she from the south, but we are both of the same ilk. She came from Madras to Bombay –

now, Chennai to Mumbai – to study art at JJ. I travelled from Kolkata to Mumbai to study journalism at XIC (Xavier Institute of Communications). When we met I was recovering from a broken relationship, and she had just dumped someone because she was bored of him. We hit it off from day one. She and I liked the same authors. Our reactions to theatre and cinema gelled. Both of us detested *bhelpuri* but liked *panipuri*. Within a year of our first meeting we decided to move-in together and rented a 1BHK in Versova.

'We were now working. Life was full for us with work and play, both in the measure we liked. We earned enough between us to get by comfortably with rare extravagances once in a while. Yes, we had to mind our expenses but it was never money that held the strings to the happiness, passion, celebration that our life together was.

'Her parents were quite distressed with our non-conformist lifestyle but Dwit didn't care.

'Six happy years we enjoyed. Sometime in the seventh year our fights began. Not that we hadn't had our bad moments earlier. Dwit and I argued constantly, but always about inconsequential or impersonal things. At times the arguments would flare up and one of us would get angry at the other. Moments later we would be laughing and cuddling each other.

'She changed, somehow. I've never understood why.'

Aditya interrupted.

'I remember Tina mentioning around Tamanna's birthday year before last, that you had resigned from Sanghavi's. September 2003. She was quite upset about it, in fact considered resigning herself. Hadn't you switched to free-lancing then? Could that have triggered the change?'

Manas looked at him in consternation.

'Yes. That would be about right. But . . . but she never objected to it. In fact . . . but no . . . I think it may have something to do with her change in attitude. I had no pay check coming in regularly. My earnings were very erratic. I thought it a minor irritation but. . . '

Manas wanted a smoke. But as even Aditya had desisted from lighting up, he concluded he had better not. He took a sip of water before continuing.

'I don't know when . . . I don't know why . . . but in that last year our fights were of a more personal nature. Gayatri . . . she began finding faults in me. I was slovenly, I smoked too much, I wasn't serious enough about life . . . She wanted us to get married, to have children. We had our most bitter fight the evening before she actually walked out on me. Gayatri. . . .

"You know how it makes me feel to beg you to marry me after seven years of living together?"

'I could see no love in her eyes then, it seemed like a deal and that I should honour it simply because it was her fair due.'

"Abar na! What is wrong with you since the past few months? Don't you trust me anymore? And you know well enough that I can't marry as of now. I have too many responsibilities. You know I am running two houses as well as funding my brother's education. . . ."

"You are running a house and a half, Manas. Do not forget that I am contributing equally to our expenditure here. For God's sake, Manas, we can't live like gypsies, we need to think of our future. At least, I need to think of my future. You can't just reject assignments because they are not interesting enough. One has to be secure to allow oneself the luxury of being choosey. What right do you have? Every rupee that you earn goes into meeting the basics and, of course, in up-keeping your all-too-dependent family."

"Are your issues with me or my family, Gayatri? If this is your attitude now, I shudder to think what you would demand of me if we were to be married. You would reduce them to nothing."

"This is what you think of me? That I would reduce them to nothing! Mother was right that you wouldn't commit. I was a fool to believe in this shitty free-love business for all these years."

"We both have enjoyed these years, Gayatri. Now that you have changed your stance, this becomes shitty? So what was this for you all along, an investment in me which now has matured and should pay its returns in marriage? Yes, I too can't believe that you are saying any of this. And by the way, you forget that for all these seven years there has been no one for me except you. What of that?"

"I am asking you one last time, are you with me in this or not? I refuse to embarrass my parents more on your account."

"Mithya katha! It is not about your parents, it is about you. They were not okay with this arrangement even seven years back. It didn't bother you then."

"Well, it does now."

"That's not my problem then. Is it, Gayatri?"

"Manas, I guess the time has then come to go our separate ways."

'At that moment I think I really did not believe that she would move out.

'At first I was angry. But then I began to miss her. Every morning I would make the tea — we both liked it without milk and sugar — and she would rustle up our usual breakfast of toast and eggs — I liked them semi-boiled and she liked them overdone. We always argued who would shower first. If we went together we would be late for work. One of us would read out the interesting bits from the newspaper and we would argue about them over breakfast. Sundays and holidays we would laze in bed and work together on the crossword puzzles in the newspapers till one of us got hungry. On breezy evenings we'd go and sit by the sea-front. Now it only made me sad. I couldn't enjoy any more the roasted corns and peanuts we had shared so often. Bus rides made me feel empty as I had no one sitting or standing with me – to be protected from sleazy elbows. At night I missed her warmth. The silence deafened me – Dwit was a great mumbler in sleep, and often snored. Going to the theatre was a bore. No one could discuss the performance as well as Dwit could.

'Without Dwit my life meant nothing. To live again I had to get her back.

'Not more than a fortnight after she left I began calling her, sms-ing her, emailing. At first she didn't respond. One night, at about 2a.m., I called her. I told her I would die without her, I would do whatever she desired, but she must come back. She just heard me out and at the end calmly told me she needed time to think and not to use emotional blackmail with her ever again, to be the man she knew me to be. She disconnected and when I tried calling again, found her mobile switched off.

'That triggered the worst asthma attack I have ever had. I was in hospital. My brother Aman, and Tina, took turns looking after me. I insisted they not inform Gayatri of my condition. I had to be a man and fight my own battle. I certainly wanted her back, but not out of pity. Those five days were the worst in my life. I battled with myself physically as well as emotionally.

'The day I returned home from the hospital I received a short sms from her: I need time.

'It took me two months to wrap up my ongoing assignments in Mumbai and set up Aman well enough to manage without me for the few months that I hoped to be away. A close friend working with the *Deccan Herald* vouched for my credentials and before I landed in Chennai I had a job, well paying and stable, just as Gayatri wanted.'

Manas nodded at Aditya as he said this. He went on.

'Full of hope and enthusiasm I boarded the train to be with the only person who could make or break my life. As the train left VT, I sms'd her: I'm coming.

'As I was exiting Chennai Central I heard a familiar voice calling out my name. Gayatri.

'We hugged. The tightness with which she held me sent a current of excitement running through me. My battle was already won. I thought. But. . . .

"*How are you now?*", Gayatri asked.

"*I am good and I am in your city. But how did you know?*"

"*So you are! I called up Aman the moment I got your cryptic message.*"

"*Cryptic! My message! You are a great one to talk, Dwit! You yourself said, "I need time"!*"

"*I was engaged to someone from my community, a distant relative's brother-in-law. He had a promising future and a pleasing personality.*"

"*Was?*"

"*I made him call it off. He was everything you are not. Well-mannered and considerate, level-headed and practical, rich and ambitious. But he liked bhelpuri and hated panipuri. He was self-conscious and meticulous. Going for a coffee, a movie . . . anything was out of the question unless it had been pre-planned. I didn't understand his Unix, he had no interest in art. Then he got this great job in the U.S. I said I had no wish to move to an alien place. By then I was bored stiff of him. And so, as easily as it had started, it ended.*"

'I thought then that all my life's woes were over, but strange are the ways of the mind and the heart. We would meet every day after work and talk. I couldn't help but delve into those weeks she had spent with another man.

What did he like most in you, Gayatri?

You must have kissed? Was he a good kisser?

Where did his hands rest when the two of you sat in a theatre?

Did you drink from the same glass?

'I was like a man possessed, who would not be at rest till he knew everything.

'Gayatri thought it would be best to have everything out in the open. That it was only right that I know it all. She answered all my questions willingly and with her usual frankness. She alternated between pangs of guilt for walking out on me and paranoia of losing me. But the more she told me the more my imagination flared. She sensed my obsession and tried to reason with me. Our quarrels began again. In the end it was she once again who put an end to our sinking relationship. After making one last final attempt. . . .

"*Manas, I am guilty, perhaps beyond pardon, for doing what I did. But the fact is that I love you and I want to be with you. Please forgive me, if not for me then for the love that we have between us. I spoilt it once, don't spoil it again.*"

"*You should not have gone, Dwit. Why was my love not enough? I can't see you, kiss you, hold you . . . without thinking of that man. I can't!*"

Her last words were, "*I understand. Perhaps it was not meant to be.*"

'I've been back in Mumbai these past ten months. We haven't spoken to each other since that last day in Chennai.

'In these months I've seen several girls with marriage in mind. I am 35 now. I want now what Gayatri had demanded of me then – a steady income, a spouse to come back to, children and that too, soon. But I still haven't found the one that's right. Some are just too stupid, some lack spontaneity, some too vain, some too gushy and all over me, some I fear would be over-dependent on me. No one has the right mix.'

Manas?'

Manas nodded.

Upasna spoke up. 'You can't find another Dwit and she couldn't find another Manas.'

'You know what Tina meant, don't you? Go to her, Manas,' Poorvi said softly.

Manas looked at his watch.

~

In the hills. . .

Tina sat down on the damp, dirty undergrowth. She unclenched her fist and held them out flat on her knees. She closed her eyes.

Tina submitted herself to her Maker. At that moment, Tina stopped existing. She was no longer aware of her body and its aches and pains; unaware of the beating heart; immune to the harsh forest. No sadness, no conflict. A total surrender.

Tina was the air in the forest, the tree under which she sat, the flower that had closed itself unseen amidst tall grass, the squirrel that lay quiet in its hollow, the bird that perched silently on a high branch. She was everything and everything was her. A singularity of existence.

37

Dear Poorvi

I couldn't own up to what 'is' and you to what you are. To say 'I can't' when the fact is 'I won't' is to deny oneself that basic starting platform of self-acceptance from which sprouts intelligent life itself. Self-deception kills slowly.
Now that I know 'things', my great wish is to accept them. It is a daily process.

Love
Tina

The others waited patiently while Poorvi stayed engrossed in the short letter for a few minutes. Finally she refolded the letter and, adjusting the pleats of the sari draped over her thighs, began speaking.

'I have always been amidst ultra . . . ultra-rich, ultra-protected and ultra-pampered. I knew I just had to lisp a whim and it would be catered to. Barbie dolls in those days were expensive imports and I had a huge collection of them with all the other paraphernalia – doll furniture, doll clothes, doll houses. Then it was tricycles and bicycles. Even if I had half a dozen friends over, we could each ride one. In my teens it was Mac make-up, Hollywood videos, pop music cassettes, jeans and t-shirts, and a private telephone in my room with no extensions. Later it was jewellery, designer outfits and accessories, perfumes and spending money. On my seventeenth birthday I was given a credit card with no spending limit. But even as I was permitted these extravagances I knew there were certain lines I could not cross. In fact I knew I couldn't even bend or stretch them.

'I belong to a rich yet conservative family whose abiding tenet across generations has been patriarchy. My grandmother submitted to my grandfather and, after he died, to my father. My mother never questioned my father's rules and decisions. So even though I did not receive less love or care than my brother, Tarang, I always knew that he of the privileged gender had liberties I did not and could never have. In fact right from early childhood I was conscious of two omnipotent influences in my life – money and my lesser gender.

'A tear in my eyes during a fight with Tarang and he would get a slap or even a thrashing while I received, at worst, a verbal reprimand. Yet while he could tease my friends – all girls – I was not allowed to mix or jest with his friends – all boys. When hints would fail I would be ordered off. My brother was going to a co-ed school but I was sent to an all-girls school. He could be allowed late nights while I had to be home by 8p.m. at the latest. Once, as teenagers, we were attending a social function with our parents where alcohol was served. Tarang took a glass but wouldn't allow me to take one. Girls don't drink, not in our families, he said. My mother happened to pass by at that moment and enquired why we were arguing and misbehaving ourselves. Tarang told her. She gave me a glare and reprimanded me severely, repeating what Tarang had said. To Tarang she only said don't drink too much.

'At religious ceremonies the male members of the family always preceded the female ones in doing the *puja*. Tarang, two years older than me, could represent my father in social functions as a Goenka, something for which my presence never sufficed. Tarang was commanded to give in to my demands for "I would get married and go away soon".

Growing up, Papa was not privy to our everyday lives. We would see him only at dinner time, when he would perfunctorily enquire how our day had gone. He would be quite satisfied with our equally succinct answers. If ever we went into details, we soon realised he wasn't paying attention. Mummy was the bridge of communication with Papa. Our demands or desires were first filtered by her and, if she thought it prudent, she would wait for the right time and opportunity to broach the matter with him. Either Dadi or Mummy was expected to handle everything. Only the most serious of matters could be taken to him. Tarang and I became experts at judging how much pressure to apply and usually backed down immediately if we realised that the matter would have to be taken to Papa.

'Mummy made up for Papa's lack of time and interest in us. With her we were garrulous, argumentative and demanding; we could even jest with her. Very soon I realized that Mummy was no less intelligent than my father. In fact I thought her more clever and versatile. He seemed only interested in business and making money whereas she could converse intelligently and knowledgably on a wider range of subjects. Often I observed her deftly manipulating his decisions to her will, and doing so in a manner whereby he felt it was his choice all along. She would usually conclude "If this is your final decision it is fine with me." I understood through Mummy that women could be in control, manipulate, and play a more powerful role than was superficially accepted; only it had to be done under a cloak. Just as Tarang was under Papa's training to handle men and money, I was under Mummy's tutelage on how to handle the man of the house, meaning my future husband.

'I had grown up observing the many contradictions around me. On festival days, especially Diwali, I marked the extravagance with which we exchanged sweet trays and boxes with families as wealthy as us. Exotic sweets and confections were packed and decorated elaborately. After we, the family, had sated our appetites the remainder was given to the household staff and the expensive frills trashed. Yet when Mummy did her accounts with the cook or the gardener she would berate them for overspending and extravagance. I often saw her ordering expensive jewellery. She wouldn't bat an eyelid over the lakhs so spent. If a servant asked for an advance it was given after much lecturing and negotiation. Money does not grow on trees, one should be prudent with one's expenses; how generous we were in that we didn't charge interest, and so on. We ate basmati rice and the staff the coarsest of varieties. Fuel prices were going up and up yet our fleet of cars ran about as much as they always had, even for the most puerile tasks. Papa never demanded we use wisdom in their usage. I overheard him complaining about the wastefulness of his office staff with the company vehicles.

'Around the time I began college I began to feel a vacuum in my life. The comforts of being in an affluent family are easily taken for granted. My insecurities were emotional. I had become intimate with a group of girls from middle class families, with working highly-educated parents. These girls enjoyed a fulsome family life where they spent many hours a day with their parents chatting, debating and discussing every subject under the sun. On holidays, while I lay sprawled in bed reading or watching television, they would be out with family. They seemed to do everything together, quite unlike the lonely world that was my lot. I was very knowledgeable on matters of fashion and style but quite ignorant when it came to politics, economics and social issues – which they could discuss with proficiency. Perhaps I knew more about the share market and real estate, and the ways of doing business; but when they debated the grey shades of Philip in Maugham's *Of Human Bondage* or of Heathcliff in *Wuthering Heights* I was totally at a loss to contribute anything to the discussion. With them I visited art exhibitions and watched cinema classics and only felt more of a peasant than a rich socialite. But with them my horizons expanded dramatically.

'My friends valued their education as a means of chalking out future careers whilst for me it had only been a done thing to get a university degree. They debated endlessly amongst themselves and with their parents various options whilst for me it was not an issue at all. My family were least interested in my university options; their only concern being that I attend a prestigious college. The only 'career' open to me was marriage to a suitable young man from an acceptable family as soon as one was identified for me by my parents. For my friends, marriage was something far away in the future, and to men of their own choosing.

'The biggest disparity between us was the way money was perceived in our respective social settings. Money for them was just a means to a good living; to us, money defined who and what we were. My friends were judicious in their spending but not overly concerned. We could spend money without much thought yet its ubiquitous power remained supreme in our minds. For them a person could be talented, intelligent, fun even if not rich; for us a person was all of this but alas, not rich.

'I sensed a certain harmony in their way of life, and it appealed to me more than the fundamentals of the lifestyle I led. Their company stimulated me. I thought I was misplaced in my setting and hungered to be a part of their world. I adopted their activities, attitudes, and priorities, and even started dressing like them – faded jeans and cotton kurtis. With them I started road-side shopping and eating street food; travelled in public transport, something which would have horrified my parents had they got wind of it; visited city libraries, institutions and landmarks. I began reading more than Page 3 of the newspapers. I had breezed through school quite happy to be an average student. Now I became serious about academics and started talking of post-graduation options. I became an active participant in their discussions and even joined various groups in college, interacting with activists and intellectuals. In my heart, I became a feminist.

'With Mummy and the other women of the clan I was free in dispensing my newly discovered opinions. With Tarang I was a little more discreet, afraid that he would tell Papa. Around my father I remained the meek and docile Poorvi. Mummy and the women, whom I would ridicule for their submissiveness, thought it a passing phase and kept my outbursts and rebellious statements hidden from him.

'What riled me was that I did not think these women to be fools. They were intelligent and wise in many ways, strategic and tactical in their manoeuvring of the men; managed large and complex households with ease and efficiency; showed great patience and fortitude. Yet they really believed themselves to be less than the men folk. To me this was unbearable. I firmly believed that women of the 21st century are equal to men.

'A brilliant female cousin received a scholarship from UGC to pursue further studies. Publicly the family boasted of their daughter's feat while privately urging her to get married. Her grandfather was in his eighties and ailing. He wished to see his great-grandson born before he went. I tried to convince her to go for the scholarship but she declined it and took great pride in her sacrifice. She got married and immediately became pregnant. It so happened my cousin's sister-in-law and I knew each other well. She herself had given birth to a girl the year before to the disappointment of her in-laws and was therefore praying anxiously for a boy. A boy it was. The family distributed *roshogollas* in silver pots. Some weeks after the birth I visited my cousin and met the sister-in-law. She was in a state of acute depression. Her in-laws openly derided her for her own failure. She may have been the elder daughter-in-law but her status had declined considerably.

'I tell you about this experience because of the influence it had on my life, though much later.

'A male cousin of mine fell in love with a Parsi girl and remained adamant about marrying her till the family ostensibly caved in but told him he should bear in mind that his rash act would lead to problems for the girls of the family, including me. He came to me with his dilemma and I told him to go ahead and follow the dictates of his heart, meaning to marry the Parsi girl. The next day I heard he had agreed to marry a girl of the family's choosing with only one condition, that he be married after the Parsi girl's own wedding. Such were the ways of preserving family name and traditions in my community.

'I zealously held forth on my outrage and frustration over such incidents. But never before the men folk, the ones who really held the reins of power. I sincerely believed that when my own time would come I would be more steadfast than my weak-kneed cousins. The opportunity to show my grit came soon enough.

'I fell in love with a man six years older, a Bengali Professor of English, Soumitra. He was a free thinker, an intellectual, and firmly believed in the equality of the sexes. He had many female admirers, many pursuers. Yet he chose me. I was flattered and exhilarated. For months we went around together. Always in complete secrecy. Only my college friends knew of my infatuation.

'Strange are the ways of the heart. Once the initial euphoria of having a young, dashing, intelligent and most coveted 'catch' as my very exclusive boyfriend ebbed, once I had explored and experimented with all that intrigued me about him, once we had settled into the routine boyfriend-girlfriend mould, I woke up to the things that were not so exhilarating about him. Whether we were eating at a roadside dhaba or in a swanky restaurant he insisted on splitting the bill. Initially it pleased me as a demonstration of his firm belief in equality of the sexes but later I began to wonder whether it was penny-pinching.

'All Soumitra ever gifted me was books or cassettes, hand-written notes and poetry penned by him. He knew of my fondness for flowers and chocolates but he considered them a waste of money. He kept a plastic bottle in his cloth *jhola* which he kept refilling during the course of the day. I drank only mineral water. He thought it a fetish of the rich. He often ridiculed people of my ilk. Initially I joined him with relish but in time it began to irk me and I would start defending my own.

'He would tease me sometimes with observations like I could match cars from the family fleet to my dress, my Omega watch could have put roofs over an entire *basti*, the amount I spent on shoes could finance a month's budget of a college professor. Where earlier I had laughed at such jibes, now I wished he at least had a non-air-conditioned jalopy rather than the open scooter on which we drove around, suffering the heat, dust and humidity; not to speak of my fear of discovery, never too far under the surface.

'He relished non-vegetarian food and I was a strict vegetarian. I could speak of art and literature for some time but soon I'd tire and consider it trivial and inconsequential. When we happened to be with his professor colleagues he usually switched to Bengali, even though he knew of my difficulty with the language. Consequently I was left out of such discussions and never invited to join in. At times I felt as if his colleagues were looking at me and thinking, '*Here comes Soumitra's fancy – a spoilt rich little girl who wants to be a part of a world she does not belong to.*'

'And so, though in my own settings I was the princess, here I was an outsider. Amongst my own I was considered smart and rebellious; in Soumitra's world I was thought average and struggling. At home I relaxed with mindless soaps on the television, romantic fiction of the Danielle Steel variety. With him I could only talk Eliot and Milton, most of which I didn't understand; or discuss world events and issues which soon bored me as being too distant from my own cloistered world. In my world I had to prove nothing with the assurance of my lineage, in his world I was always under challenge. The pressure had begun to stress me out. I had begun to restrict our meetings to shorter and shorter time spans, saying I needed time on my own, or, was required at home. Such partings always concluded with his jibes ringing in my ears.

'In my more serious moods, I wondered about our relationship. Did I really want the kind of life he could offer? His father's hospitalisation cleared my mind.

'He tried to dissuade me from visiting the hospital. I went anyway. All my earlier visits to a medical facility had been to private rooms and suites in upmarket nursing homes. I was ill-prepared for the horrors that assailed me visiting the general ward of a government-run hospital. The hospital was swarming with people through whom I passed reluctantly, much afraid of contacting an illness myself. I couldn't turn back now. I tried to minimise any contact with the hordes but frequently was forced to brush past them.

'He had given me a ward number. It took me five minutes to locate the ward but it seemed like the most horrendous five minutes of my life. What hit me at first glance was the utter gracelessness of the stark surrounding. Ugly wrought iron beds with paint peeling from every possible joint peeped at me from the sagging thin mattresses. There were many more people than beds. Some patients seemed to be stretched out on the dirty stained linoleum of the floor on dirty stained sheets that had perhaps once been white. Many patients seemed to have flocks of their relatives or friends around them. The only way I distinguished patient from visitor was by the hospital gowns the patients wore. They all seemed equally wasted, unkempt and unhealthy to my unaccustomed eyes.

'I couldn't place his father in the multitude. I identified a hospital attendant by his uniform of white shirt over striped shorts – what I would expect a jail inmate to wear. From him I got a number. I looked around me with puzzlement. There seemed to be no rooms in the ward. Then it dawned on me that what I had been given was a bed number. I found him occupying a bed at the far end of the ward, covered with a worn-out sheet that, though starched and clean, bore impressions of earlier patients who must have bled upon it. The rickety side table was coated with dust and caked with grime. On it I saw a cheap plastic hand fan which I picked up gingerly and fanned alternatively over his father and myself, trying to swat away the flies and mosquitoes hovering at will over us. I looked around at the other visitors, at their crumpled taat saris, at the plastic bangles on their wrist, at their humble belongings – small tiffin containers; refilled Bisleri bottles; thermoses with cracked lids; napkins as faded, old and tired as their faces; at their tiny purses from which some extracted crumpled and filthy five or ten rupee notes . . . it all seemed to be from a world I had glimpsed only in the arty movies Soumitra liked to take me to.

'That day after my return from the hospital I understood how deep one's roots are. I realised that I did not detest money or the comforts it bought but the license it gave to the women to do nothing. I deduced that ideals of frugality, purpose-in-life and industriousness appear beautiful in conversations but are not so pretty in real life. Soumitra and I belonged to two very different worlds. I felt deeply for him but it would not suffice to keep the relationship happy and comfortable. I had to wriggle out of this situation. And I knew how to do so without revealing the shallowness of my reasons for doing so. Yes, I didn't have the gall to own up to my own motives for the decision.'

Poorvi had spoken non-stop for a long time. The others waited silently while she sipped some water from her glass. Finally she cleared her throat and continued with her story.

'Soumitra's father slipped into a coma soon after my visit. It was two weeks before we had an opportunity to meet and talk. I told him now that I had graduated, my family was pressurising me to get married. I would have to tell them something. He said in view of his father's condition and the precariousness of his finances the question of marriage just didn't arise at that juncture. I offered him monetary help. As expected he declined. I remember his words then. He said "I doubt I will be in a situation to consider marriage in the near future. I love you immensely, Poorvi, but can't expect you to wait endlessly for me. Perhaps it is time for us to call it quits." We wished each other luck and parted with a hug. Never once did he remind me of my earlier utterances of being the mistress of my own life. That was the last we saw of each other.

'The only condition I imposed upon my family was that I would only marry someone based outside Kolkata. I met and liked Avinash who lived in Mumbai. During our engagement period I told him about Soumitra, assuring him that it was a closed chapter. He admitted he himself had had relationships in the past. The matter ended there. We got married and I moved to Mumbai.

'Avinash was the eldest of two brothers so I was assured of my seniority in the pecking order of daughter-in-laws. The family is a Mumbai institution with wealth going back many generations. They are conservative without being unbearably so. What they had lacked was style. Within months of my marriage I was the toast of the house, the toast of all who knew us, for my flair and style. My in-laws were in awe of me.

'Soon I was immersed in the very world I had ridiculed earlier. Whenever my inner voice happened to chastise me I would visit a local NGO and salve my conscience with a hefty donation. I assured myself that this was just a necessary phase in my life; the realities were not forgotten, merely postponed for an indeterminate future. I had duties and responsibilities to my new family that needed to take precedence over my own desires and needs.

'After our second anniversary the suggestions and innuendos started to fly thick and fast. It was time to consider motherhood. Avinash's mother and grandmother seemed visibly disturbed each time I got my periods. Before long, other relatives and family friends too started goading me, to give the family an heir.

'Avinash had always assured me that, to start a family, we could wait as long as I wanted. One night I told him I was ready.

He asked me if I was sure. I told him about his mother's wishes and that I felt it was my duty to give the family an heir. His pleasure at this was apparent. I took heart; rising up in his esteem was worth it.

'Aanya happened and I wanted to make a point to the world that my first born, even though a girl, was as much welcome as a boy would have been. Her birth was celebrated with as much pomp and glamour, as much extravagance, as was possible. I felt a little guilty at the obscene amount I was spending, that it could have been used for a far worthier cause. I assured myself that it was justified, not only because Avinash's parents wanted to celebrate the birth of their first grandchild, but because of the message that I emphatically sent out to the world – that I believed in true equality of the sexes.

'Avinash's brother got engaged. All arrangements for the ceremonies were left to my discretion as my in-laws by now had complete faith in my acumen at organising grand events. It went as expected and I got oodles of praise from Avinash, my in-laws, the relatives and friends of the family, and even the new *sambandhis*.

'Life moved on. Tarana, my second daughter was born. I was sorely disappointed inwardly at not having had a boy. My in-laws showed no such regrets. They expressed the wish to celebrate her birth as they had Aanya's. Avinash knew me well enough by now to guess my inner disappointment. Handing the baby to me he whispered in my ears that he had clinched a major deal that day, Lakshmi had entered their house. Seeing the cherubic princess in my arms all my doubts vanished and I was overwhelmed with love for her.

'Everything changed for me after Aman, Avinash's nephew, was born. With his birth my status in the family underwent a subtle but sure change. From being the loved but relatively insignificant *choti bahu* my sister-in-law became the undeclared future mistress of the clan, the one who would one day be in custody of the keys that dangled smugly from my mother-in-law's waist. Where she had just been informed on major matters, now her opinion was sought, and given as much weight as mine. I continued to represent the family in social gatherings but, within the four walls of our house, it became increasingly clear to me that in time she would be the one calling the shots. She herself seemed stumped with this unwanted new attention. She neither wanted to be the baton carrier nor did she feel herself equipped to handle the limelight. She would tell me "Bhabhi, you are the one with the know-how and tact, not me. I'd rather be in your shadow." She was such a sweet and simple soul that I knew she meant it.

'Avinash was quite happy with two children and didn't feel the need for a son. But I was besotted with the idea. I convinced him we should try again. I got pregnant. A surreptitious sonography with an agreeable doctor revealed the foetus to be a girl. I was devastated. I wanted a termination of the pregnancy. Time was of the essence. I knew the family were dead against the very idea of abortion. I flew into a rage with Avinash as he tried to convince me otherwise. My mother-in-law proposed the idea of adoption in case I was so dead set on a son. Avinash supported the notion. I screamed at him "I wonder if she would advise the same to her daughter. She obviously thinks I have no other business in life than to produce and nurture children one after the other. She is just a tenth pass, what more can be expected out of her!" Avinash quietly told me it was I who wanted a boy, not them, and left the room. He had left behind something on the bed. It was a CD I had noticed him carrying earlier.

'The CD was a clinical documentation of what a foetus goes through during the termination process. The forceps are used to grab one of the extremities of the child to pull it off, literally dismembering it. There was an abortionist describing the procedure, who said, "We know the foetus is still alive, either because we can feel it move or we actually see a heart beat as we're starting the procedure."

'Can there be anything more heinous a human can do to another . . . and that to not just 'another' but to one's own flesh and blood?

'I am a murderess.'

Aditya was unable to restrain himself.

'What rubbish! Accept your need, even if it's silly! Just adopt a boy.'

~

In the hills. . .

Tup, tup, tup. Cool drops fell on her skin . . . her eyelashes . . . like the rain, Tina's tears fell.

And like the strengthening downpour, her eyes shed heavy tears.

Thunderous claps found their echo within her tormented soul. Like flashes of lightning, Tina saw glimpses of the life she had lived.

Mist engulfed her. The clouds hugged the earth. Tina wrapped her arms about herself. Then, as she looked up, the sky opened and a golden orb appeared. She held out her arms and again opened her palms. A cool refreshing breeze sprang up as Tina felt the last vestiges of Aditya leave her.

I am free!

From a distance Tina could see a lovely flower, the first rays of the sun glinting off the pearly drops kissing its soft petals . . . a squirrel scampering past . . . the crickets were back, noisily seeking their mates . . . a colouful butterfly flitted onto her sleeve and stayed there, gently fluttering its wings . . . a green flash of a pair of parrots racing between trees. The leaves fluttered. The wet earth perfumed the air as a soft wind blew. Puddles mirrored the sky.

Yes, Nature is telling me life has its inevitable course. Night and day. Darkness and sunshine. Going and coming. There is no holding on, no constant. Aditya needed me for that phase in his life. When he needed me no more, I pined for him and made myself miserable. When the time comes, one must let go and await the break in the clouds.

Like the rapidly clearing sky, her thoughts flowed clear as rain-washed air.

I am free of you, Aditya!

Her peals of happy laughter rang out in the awakened forest. A passionate desire coursed through her.

I want to create, be, do, without an inherent conflict.

She pulled out her camera and started clicking.

She clicked a deer nursing its calf . . . a slug that was on its way to find a new home . . . the serpentine queue of ants at their task once again after the hiatus . . . the seven-coloured rainbow extending from one end to the other . . . a puddle that reflected the sky and then bent down to look into it more closely. She saw her own reflection in it . . . hair unkempt, scratches all over, puffed eyes, red nose, swollen lips . . . yet. . . .

I look beautiful. I was never not beautiful. . . .

She clicked her own reflection.

There was no stopping her after that. Everywhere she looked, she saw eternity, wholeness, hope and joy. Her eyes sought and found, fingers clicked and captured.

Tina couldn't stop smiling, and all the while, she thanked the Maker for all the beauty that He had so generously bestowed on

His creatures which she could appreciate only now. She stopped clicking only when the batteries ran out.

As she told Prashant later, "I could create. Wholeness was not just outside, it was within me too. . . ."

BOOK 4

BOOK 4

38

The blaring horns, the cacophony of revving engines, the dust and heat of a dry June day as Gurgaon awaited the arrival of the monsoon, none of this impinged on Upasna's mind as she sat quiescently in the autorickshaw lost in thought. She was planning the day ahead. The sudden jerk as the gearless vehicle shot forward with the green light loosened her grip on the satchel lying in her lap. It would have fallen on the dirty un-upholstered floor but she quickly grabbed it. Looking up her eyes chanced upon the huge hoarding across the road. A new Barbie doll was being launched. She grimaced as her mind flew back to the day she had walked out of her husband's house.

It was the morning of the Sunday after she had returned from Mahabaleshwar. Passing through the large central hall that served as the family room in the big house she saw Shanay playing with Priya, her sister-in-law's daughter, who was over for the weekend. Lakshmibai, her maid, was dusting in the room. Upasna smiled, seeing her son playing with dolls.

Shanay twisted both the arms of the doll behind its back. 'You know I hate double crease on my trousers. I don't want it repeated again.'

Upasna froze mid-step. An exasperated Priya was saying 'She is not the Mummy, stupid! You are daddy, I am Mummy, and these two Barbies are our girls.' She went on, 'Shanay, this girl doesn't want to go school today. She says her tummy is hurting.' To Upasna, her son seemed to be exactly mimicking his father's didactic tone as he retorted, 'Just give her one tight slap and pack her off to school.'

Upasna's eyes locked with Lakshmibai's. The woman's ancient eyes were full of pity. Upasna did not scold Shanay. What would have been the point? Like grandfather, like father, like son. She reached a decision. Indicating to Lakshmibai that she should follow, Upasna went to her room. Umesh was at his club.

An hour later she left the house with Shanay. Umesh had not yet returned home. Her in-laws were also out.

The autorickshaw had stopped. The driver was saying, 'Memsaab!'

It seemed she was early. The office was empty except for the peon who nodded at her and went back to his newspaper. Sitting at her desk she again started reminiscing.

She had not gone to Kolkata, to her parents' house. Instead she had gone to a friend's place. A little later Umesh had called on her cellphone. He was almost incoherent in his anger. Upasna remained calm, cool, collected, while speaking little.

'I will not allow my son to become another Umesh,' she had told him.

'You women have no common sense. Cocooned in your father's shell then your husband's, you know nothing of the world. You think you can earn enough to sustain your newfound independence? There are thousands of MBAs crawling all over like ants. You will be one of them too.'

'I will manage.'

'Go running back to daddy dearest to feed yourself.'

'*I am not going back to my father's house. Ever!*'

'*Upasna, you will be begging at my door in a month's time. If not earlier!*'

'*We will see.*'

'*Then you will get a treatment worse than what you are walking out on. Remember that.*'

'*You don't scare me any more. I have taken away that power from you.*'

'*I will not allow you to take Shanay from me!*'

'*The courts will decide.*'

Umesh had disconnected.

The EPABX in the main office started buzzing. Upasna watched the peon move unhurriedly to answer the phone. He was mumbling something on the mouthpiece then looked up at her. He pressed some keys and the extension at her desk started ringing.

'Upi?'

'Hi Tinee!'

'As per my reckoning you have accumulated sufficient leave. Pack you bags, girl. You're coming over to Mahabaleshwar. . .'

The cousins had kept up with each other, though they had not met in a long time.

'. . .Suniti will come over to look after Shanay. I'll be there.'

'Upi, cannot wait to see you!'

'Me too Tinee'.

39

'Come in', said Kriya to an almost inaudible knock. The girl walked in petite, unsure, apprehensive.

'Good morning, Ma'am. I'm Shefali Kavia. We met at the NEXT convocation last week. Ma'am, you asked me to see you today, Saturday. I had exhibited jewellery, purses and other trinkets done in shades of brown in metal and clay, Ma'am.' She said it all in one breath as if she had rehearsed it a hundred times before stepping into Kriya's office.

'Yes, of course I remember you. Take a seat, Shefali. If I remember correctly you used a mixture of clay, copper, and coloured stones.'

The girl's delight at being remembered showed on her face.

'Yes, Ma'am.'

'Passing out on NEXT's Merit List is very creditable. Your instructors said you have a natural talent. Very creative.'

The girl relaxed visibly. Kriya smiled at her; she was thinking the girl reminded her of Smita.

'So tell me, Shefali, how or where did this inspiration come from?'

Kriya interviewed the girl for half an hour. At the end of it she was sure Shefali was a genuine talent, raw and unpolished, but very promising.

'Shefali, would you like to join our establishment?'

'Oh, Ma'am! Of course I would. You've been my idol for years. It's been my dream to work for you one day.'

'You'll have to work hard you know. I run a very tight ship.'

'No, Ma'am! I mean . . . yes Ma'am, I'll give it not my 100% but my 200%.'

Kriya smiled and said, 'That's exactly the kind of spirit we welcome here! Can you begin from Monday?'

'Today, Ma'am. I can start right away.'

Kriya laughed at the girl's ebullience and leaning forward patted her hand.

'Today we'll induct you and you can begin working from Monday.'

She buzzed her secretary on the intercom.

'Laura, I'm sending Shefali to you. Induct her today please. She'll be coming from Monday. Assign her to the Smita Sharma line. Accessories for the fall collection. Familiarise her with the theme. Give her whatever material she asks for, I'm giving her some homework.'

'Shefali, sketch some accessories – at least twenty different patterns to go with the upcoming theme. We will meet in about 4-5 days. Laura will give you everything you need. One more thing, you can shift your belongings to our guesthouse till you can make alternate arrangements. Your payroll has started. Welcome to KC, Shefali.'

'Thank you, Ma'am. You are like God to me.'

'We are all humans here and let us keep it that way, okay.' Kriya grinned at her to take away the edge from her words.

Once Shefali left, Kriya pulled out the photograph of Smita and herself taken on the day of their own convocation at NEXT so many years ago. It had been found on Smita's bedside table, near her body.

Smita, she is so much like you.

Their last conversation was etched in Kriya's mind.

She had not managed to persuade Smita to go to the *filmwallah*. There had been a show-down. A weeping Smita had told Kriya she didn't want her own label, that she would be quite happy to work for Kriya as a mere designer with no public recognition.

'Smita, the creative life of a fashion designer is short and limited. Trends change. People get bored. The fashion industry periodically demands an infusion of fresh blood. Do you think designs sell? It is marketing that sells. You are now a spent creative force. Your designs no longer matter. They are in fact out-dated and useless. You think I'm giving you your own label because of your originality? You can't be such a fool, Smita! I consider you my friend and confidante. The label would be your reward for the years of friendship you have given me. And anyway, I have spent a great deal of time, effort and money in preparation for the Smita Sharma label. It's too late to dump it now.'

'B-but Kriya! Don't make me go to that man!'

'Since when have you become so prudish, Smita!'

'P-please, I implore you!'

Kriya had become angry then.

'If you think that I am exploiting you, you are free to leave.'

'Kriya, I think no such thing. I want to work with you. I have done whatever you asked me to do all these years, even when I thought it wrong. But this is not about me, it is about you.

I thought it wrong. But this is not about me, it is about you. You do not need to be petty. You can afford to be generous and compassionate. Kriya, you are blessed that you have not had to fight for your basic needs. You are in a position to help others. You do so, but the price that you ask from them drains their very soul.'

For a mere moment Kriya's jaw dropped. It was the first time ever that timid Smita had said so much. *And in the English that had been my gift to her!*

Kriya let go. All her self-restraint vanished as she launched into a tirade.

'What do you have in you, you middle-class, small-town idiot! A little talent that would have led you nowhere without my support and promotion. You would have been working in some piddling fashion house with a hundred others at a salary that would have been a fraction of what you send home every month. Or perhaps you would have opened a wretched little tailoring unit stitching blouses.

'You were good because I gave you the tools to be good. It is I who sculpted you, educated you, and made you what you are today. The self-confidence that gives you the audacity to speak like this to me is a result of my charity. You couldn't speak a sentence without stuttering before. Oh, you were not even fit enough to be present during client meets, tacky and gauche that you were. Because of my compassion you didn't have to worry about your basic needs, or those of your impoverished family. I practically nursed your father for three months. What price did I demand for it?'

She gave Smita an ultimatum. Either she went or she was out of a job. Kriya shredded every last vestige of self-respect in the pleading Smita.

'No one will employ a has-been designer! I, Kriya, will ensure it. I have considerable clout in the fashion industry. Get out of my sight now. Go home and think about it. If you go this evening, I'll forgive your ungratefulness and you can come to work tomorrow. If not, you can go hang yourself for all I care!'

Smita, I promise you this girl will not suffer the way you did. I will ensure that in five years she will have her own label.

Kriya's cellphone rang. It was Tina. Kriya had a hard time containing her tears. It was a while before she could manage to speak.

'Tina, I still don't get how you knew. But that evening in Mahabaleshwar has been my saviour. After Smita's news, killing myself seemed to be my only redemption. But I couldn't do it. That would only have been an easy escape. No salvation at all. I thought I must live and suffer. It was hell. Then you showed me the way.

'Our flagship label is now Smita Sharma. Under it I promote fresh and deserving talent. Today I chose another debutant.

'Tina, I have five fresh pages in my album so far, including today's. And many many new photographs!'

'Kriya, I'm happy. I guess we are truly never completely lost.'

'Hey, girl! I have just been ranting about myself. Since that queer though brilliant letter I've been aching to meet you. And how are you?' Kriya asked.

'I am good, better than I have ever been Kriya. You will hear it all. . .'

Tina invited Kriya to Mahabaleshwar. . . .

40

Manas was typing an email to Aman.

'Bravo, brother! The 'appearance' allele in our gene pool will now flower with her beauty. I hope you haven't coerced her into submission! Jokes apart, Aman, I am mighty glad for you. You should tell Baba and Ma about her now. They will be so relieved that at least one son is being sensible, having given up on me. There's no reason to delay, especially as you have also been promoted and seem set for an illustrious career. They are getting old, Aman. It is good that now you have a Mediclaim entitlement that can also cover them. Illnesses are unpredictable things and one must provide for them.

I can see you laughing, reading this. Yes, Aman, I can understand now what Dwit meant. All her words then together now ring true. She had grown up and I hadn't.

By the way, she sends you her love. I got an email from her the other day. The baby's doing fine. They have moved into their new flat. All three of them take a stroll in Central Park every evening, weather permitting. She's still thrilled by New York. Oh! She got that job she was after in some art gallery. Starts in a month or so.

I should be going now. Else again the canteen will run out of dal. These journalists really have a healthy appetite.

Hey! I have an idea! Does she have an elder sister, or even a cousin? For then I wouldn't have to do any homework and we could get married under the same pandal.

Take care and tell her Manas Da welcomes her wholeheartedly to the family.

Love, Da.'

Manas didn't really feel hungry. He remained seated at his desk. Through the glass wall of the cabin he could see he was alone in the vast office. He removed his shoes, put his feet up on the glass-topped desk, and leaned back in his executive chair, its springs groaning under him.

He recalled that day when he had caught a night bus from Mahabaleshwar to Mumbai and got down at the airport to catch the first morning flight to Chennai.

He had been waiting for her when she arrived at her office.

Snips of the scene played out in his mind.

Without any preliminaries he uttered, 'Marry me, Dwit. Right now.'

She looked him in the eye and shook her head. 'No.'

'It's over, Manas. No, don't interrupt. Hear me out first.

'At first I was beside myself with grief when you left. But then, as time went by, I thought deep and hard on our relationship. Those years we were together we were so juvenile in our optimism. We just flowed along, allowed ourselves to be carried by the tide, with no thought of growing old. Our relationship was like your smoking, an accustomed habit. That last year I had changed but you hadn't. I began worrying about the future. You couldn't understand.

'Perhaps Manas we were both too volatile, too crazy, too intense to give each other lasting happiness.'

'*I love you for what you are Manas. I will always treasure the years we had together. But that's all they'll ever be: happy memories.*

'*I've met a man whom I've come to love and admire. We're getting married soon and then we're moving to America. It's over, Manas. Let go.*'

The telephone on Manas's desk began ringing shrilly,

Through sheer habit his hand reached out and plucked it from its cradle. He was about to place it back when he heard the familiar voice, 'Manas?'

'Tina!'

'Yes.'

'Durgo! Where have you been? I've been worried stiff about you. No one had any news of you. Not even your parents.'

'My sabbatical is over, Manas. I cannot say that I have found myself but I am certainly more at peace than I have ever been. How are *you?*'

Manas understood Tina's tacit question.

'I'm fine, Tina. After Mahabaleshwar I rushed to Chennai. She turned me down. Dwit's married and living in New York now. He's a good man. He'll give her the order, security and comfort that is her due. They're happy together. '

'Oh! I'm sorry, Manas.'

'Don't be, Tina. She isn't mine but I'm happy for her. This must be love. Are you in Mumbai? When do we meet?'

'No, I'm in Mahabaleshwar. I called for a reunion. All of us. Same place, same date, same time . . . just a different year. No letters. Can you come?'

'Even Mahakali couldn't keep me away! I will be there.'

41

A hundred odd voices chanted 'Heepie budday to you! Heepie budday dear Rahi!' to the drumbeats of the monsoon rain lashing the tin roof of the large community hall perched on a hilltop in the middle of the vast sprawling slum.

One-year-old Rahi though did not comprehend much, and for the most part hid behind his mother's dupatta.

'Why are they singing so funnily, mommy? They say birthday budday, just like Bai does.' Tarana tugged at Poorvi's dupatta and looked at her with her curious, five year old eyes. Bai was their domestic help.

'They do not know English, Taru, and have probably mugged the lines as you would perhaps a nursery rhyme in a strange language. That's why they sound so different,' Poorvi whispered to her.

'But then why do they sing in English?' Tarana asked yet again.

'Mmm, it is their way of thanking us, in a language they can neither speak nor understand but know that we do.' Tarana's expression changed from distaste to awe.

Poorvi, Aanya and Tarana spent a delightful hour playing games, singing songs, with the children. The roof was leaking at a couple of places but no one minded the odd drops dampening their clothes or plopping on their happy faces. Then it was time for the cake. Poorvi had arranged a vast chocolate cake for the party in the shape and style of the Vrindavan gardens near Mysore. There was much ooh-ing and aah-ing as the splendid colourful cake was unveiled. Some of the children couldn't resist the temptation and dipped their fingers in the soft confection and licked the chocolate sticking to their fingers. Poorvi pretended she hadn't seen. She held a plastic knife in Rahi's little fingers and made a cut in the cake. The feast began with Poorvi and the other elders manning the community centre serving out the samosas, bhel-puri and cake to the milling children. Aanya and Tarana also ate. For once they had been allowed to eat with their fingers and they relished the opportunity.

The party ended with a distribution of small gifts to each of the children. Then it was time to go. Fortunately the rain had stopped and they didn't get wet as they splashed through the puddles to their car parked at the end of the narrow alley that snaked down the small hill.

As they neared the car Poorvi's cellphone rang. She put Rahi in Aanya's lap and answered it. It was Tina.

'I can hear so much around you, Poorvi. Where are you, in another highbrow birthday party of the son of so-and-so?' Tina teased.

Poorvi laughed. 'No, Tina. At my own son Rahi's birthday party in Dharavi.'

'Your son?'

'Yes, Tina. I adopted him from an orphanage when he was just a week old. He had been left at its gates. Avinash and his parents, not to forget Avinash's grandmother, dote upon him. He's sitting right now in Aanya's lap gurgling away happily as Tarana tickles his little toes. Avinash's brother insisted we must have a party at home too. His wife is organising it. So you could say I'm party hopping.'

Aanya interrupted, 'Mommy, even I want to celebrate my birthday here and do my home party too. Can I do both?'

'Yes, sweetheart, we can do both!'

Poorvi brought Tina up to date on the happenings in her life.

'Tina, I have finally found a niche for myself between the idealist that I could never be and the shallow being that I was. I am finally as good as I can be. How have you been, Tina? It's been so long!'

Tina told her about the reunion.

Epilogue

10 July 2007

Evenings in Mahabaleshwar are pleasant year round but in the wet monsoon months the hills take on a magical quality. The mist engulfs the hills in a lover's embrace; yellow and orange wildflowers dot the lush and green, grassy slopes. With most hotels shut for the wet season the place takes on a calm solitude.

Prashant particularly loved this season of quietude. Walking into Aditya's old bungalow he brushed the soles of his sandals on the coir mat. From inside could be heard the voices of the others.

The friends — Kriya, Upasna, Poorvi, Manas and Tina — were in the verandah, sitting around the wooden table on the cane chairs. They greeted Prashant effusively. He smiled to himself. The last time he had met them, Tina's friends had been sombre. From Tina, who had been based in Mahabaleshwar since her separation and subsequent divorce from Aditya, he had learnt of the changes their lives had undergone in the past two years. They had every reason to be happy.

Tina was speaking, continuing from where she had broken off to greet Prashant.

'Aditya wanted me to have this house as part of our settlement. He said he already had a house here – Prat's place.'

Manas asked, 'So your divorce is final! Marry me, Tina!'

All laughed, Tina loudest of all.

'What about the girls, Tina?' Poorvi enquired.

'Shaswati and Tamanna are in a boarding school nearby Pune. They spend most of their holidays with me but visit Aditya whenever they wish to, or whenever he wants them to.'

'You are planning on restarting work any time soon, Tina?' Kriya asked.

'Well, the past year and a half or so I have been travelling with my Nikon, capturing facets of the natural world as and when they appealed to me. A few months back, at Prashant's bidding, I mailed some of my work to National Geographic. They used some of the photographs and I began freelancing for them. Then, just as I began getting 'us' together for this reunion, I received an email from an editor of the magazine seeking a more substantial arrangement with me. They asked if I was interested in becoming a permanent staffer for the magazine. They made it clear in their email that I could continue to be based in Pune.

'They asked if I was interested,' Tina said, a broad smile lighting up her face.

Sounds of more cheering reverberated in the ancient villa as glasses clinked to celebrate the good news.

Prashant of course was aware of the offer, and of Tina's acceptance of it.

Glasses clinked as Tina's friends toasted her success. Each of them, too, had cause to celebrate. Conversation moved from one to the other as they brought each other up to date on the intervening two years since their last gathering.

He smiled to himself studying Manas.

The man has certainly cleaned himself up – not just in his appearance but in his demeanour, too. The beard suits him, gives him an air of gravitas. Quite the successful television personality! Tina is right. There's no sign of grieving in him. He has made his peace with Dwit – quaint name!

His eyes moved on to Upasna.

Hmm. She doesn't hide herself any more. The long sleeves and out-size sunglasses are gone. She sits erect and proud. Definite confidence there. The moral support she got from her own family must have helped. Good of them to move to Gurgaon to be near her.

He examined Poorvi closely, noting her white cotton salwar kameez , the big white *bindi* on her forehead, the trail of vermillion disappearing into the parting of her hair.

No more of those heavy baubles weighing her down . . . skin seems to have cleared up . . . all in all a living allegory of cleansing. . . .

At that moment Poorvi was speaking.

'. . . met Soumitra after thirteen years. I told him the truth, set him free.'

Prashant turned to Kriya. Their eyes locked. Kriya spoke.

'I believe you met my father recently in Pune. He told me he asked you to write his biography.'

She laughed.

'I had a statue of a Laughing Buddha in my office. All these years I didn't dare move it. It had been put there by the great Mr Kasthiya. I finally got rid of it, sold it to an antique collector for a small fortune, and donated it all to charity. My father was livid when I told him . . .You know, it doesn't hurt me any more, that I'm not his Princess . . . So are you writing it – the biography?'

Prashant shook his head. His eyes twinkled.

'No. I have plans for a novel of my own. . . .'